Andy,

Hope you enjoy the book.

Paul Mila

4/13/04

DANGEROUS WATERS

Undersea adventure in the deep blue of the Pacific and the Caribbean

A Novel
By Paul J. Mila

authorHOUSE

1663 LIBERTY DRIVE, SUITE 200
BLOOMINGTON, INDIANA 47403
(800) 839-8640
www.authorhouse.com

First published by AuthorHouse 03/30/04

ISBN: 1-4184-0921-9 (e)
ISBN: 1-4184-0919-7 (sc)

Library of Congress Control Number: 2004091432

Printed in the United States of America
Bloomington, Indiana

This book is printed on acid-free paper.

Dedications

To my parents, Rose and Octavio,
Who instilled a love of reading in me, and lit the fire of curiosity

To Carol, Christine and Laura,
for their support and encouragement

And to Alison,
Who introduced me to the amazingly exciting and beautiful world under the sea

Acknowledgments

*I would like to thank all those who read the original
manuscript, and whose comments, suggestions and editing
made significant improvements to the final book.
Any remaining errors and shortcomings are totally the fault of
the author.*

Florence Asciolla *Tony Bliss* *Beth Bitetto*
Martha Braizbolt *Richard Callian* *Tom Carey*
Laura Carmody *Carol Catalano* *Cathleen Conforti*
Terry Gallogaly *Marilyn Holland* *Mark Lyons*
Lisanne Lange *Carol Mila* *Leon Rutman*

Technical assistance relating to scuba diving:
*Alison Dennis, Owner/Operator of ScubaWithAlison.
www.scubawithalison.com*

Technical assistance relating to police procedures:
*Lieutenant Alan Catalano, Lake Success
Police Department, Retired.*

*Police Officer John E. Galvin, New York City
Police Department, Retired.*

Part 1

Beginnings

The location of the Channel Islands, off the California coast

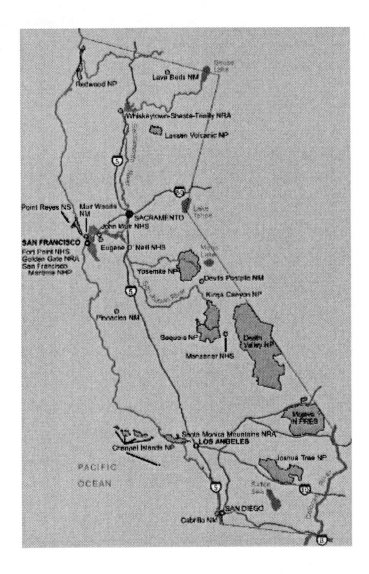

Source: California National Park Guide; map in public domain.

Chapter 1.

Santa Barbara, California

It was 6 o'clock in the morning and Terry Hunter was sitting alone on the stern of the *Catalina II,* the research vessel owned by the University of California, Santa Barbara's, Department of Marine Science. She enjoyed losing herself in her thoughts, looking at the ocean just before sunrise, when, if conditions were just right, the water resembled a black mirror, broken occasionally by a fish or some other creature busily beginning its own day. The early-morning mist coming off the water made the gentle sea breeze a bit too cool for comfort, so she was wearing a hooded sweatshirt to fend off the pre-dawn chill. Terry folded her arms and shouted down the hatch leading to the galley, "Hey, the crew could use some hot coffee up here!"

"One hot coffee on the way up!" yelled Mark Stafford as he bounded up the steps of the ladder to the main deck with two steaming cups of jo.

As Terry reached for the hot coffee, Mark pulled it back. "Kiss for the cook first."

"OK, even though you're late with the brew," Terry said, reaching up and pulling Mark's head closer and kissing him firmly on his lips, "I really need that coffee!" As their lips parted and Mark handed Terry the coffee, their eyes locked and, as lover's eyes do, spoke more about how they felt about each other than words ever could. She stood up and, as Mark watched her walk across the deck as she sipped her hot coffee, he thought, *Man, I am the luckiest guy in the world!* Terry was not only intelligent, with a sharp sense of humor, but also was one of the most beautiful women he had ever met, with shoulder-length auburn hair, attractively cut, with feathered bangs falling across green eyes and a well-tanned, athletic body; tall, with the toned muscles of a swimmer. She was also a very accomplished scuba diver, which was one reason why Mark had asked her to accompany him on this trip.

Terry was currently on track to get her Master's degree in Marine Science at U. Cal, Santa Barbara, but was still undecided about her future career plans. Mark had already completed his graduate degree program in Ecology, Evolution and Marine Biology, and had taken a teaching position at UCSB immediately after graduation. He was focusing his latest research on shark behavior, occasionally publishing articles on such topics as reproduction, indicators of aggressive behavior and the like. They had met at college and, after a brief relationship, realized that they were meant to be together.

Terry had moved into Mark's apartment two years ago and over that time, as their relationship evolved, they became best friends, confidants, and lovers. Their love grew and deepened as they continued to share experiences together, especially diving. It was as if salt water nurtured their relationship, just as fresh water causes flowers to blossom and grass to grow. They spoke frequently of their future together, which they both assumed would one day lead to marriage and children. They could not even contemplate ever being with anyone else. In each other, they had found their perfect life-partner.

Mark had initiated a project at the university that would either validate or invalidate certain assumptions about shark behavior relating to the interactions of sharks and divers. Specifically, he wanted to formally document and publish new research about earlier assumptions drawn from the experience of divers who had spent considerable time observing and interacting with various species of sharks in the wild. Their experience suggested that, when approached by sharks, the best odds for avoiding an attack came from being aggressive — not aggressive in violating the shark's personal space, but when the shark violated a diver's personal space, confronting the animal and aggressively poking, pushing or prodding it with a firm object such as a pole, spear, or even a broomstick studded with nails. Mark wanted to take it a step further, proposing that one could survive not only a short encounter in this way but also maintain one's self for an extended period of time in the presence of one or more sharks.

The project would entail traveling to the Channel Islands for a week to dive with sharks, utilizing shark cages as a safety measure. There would be a team of four divers: two divers would be in the water with sharks and exit and enter the cage throughout the dives, depending on conditions such as visibility, number of sharks and the level of aggressive behavior exhibited by the sharks. The other two divers would document the dive with still photos and video.

As they sipped their coffee watching the sunlight spill out over the water, Mark asked, "Happy the way things went last night?"

"Yes, very much so," said Terry, "Your parents are great people." Mark and Terry had preceded the other members of the research team by a couple of days so they could visit Mark's parents. For Mark, it was a good opportunity to spend some extra time visiting his parents, for the first time with Terry. Terry had been apprehensive but also excited, both about the chance to dive with sharks and especially to meet Mark's parents. As it turned out, Mark's parents, Angela and Mark Stafford senior, fell in love with Terry from the moment they met her.

In a quiet moment in his parent's kitchen, Mark's mother whispered a question in her son's ear. He smiled and pulled a small jewelry box out of his pocket and showed his mother the engagement ring he planned to give to Terry at the conclusion of the trip. Mark's mother smiled approvingly and kissed him. After their two-day visit, the drive — from Mark's parent's home to the harbor where they met the research boat that would take the team out to the Channel Islands — had been short and uneventful.

After finishing their coffee, Terry and Mark spent time straightening up and organizing equipment on the boat, waiting for the rest of the team to arrive later in the morning. As they completed their preparations, Mark glanced impatiently at his watch. It was already noon and he had wanted to be out on the water by 1 o'clock. Finally, at 12:30, Mark heard squealing tires as a mini-van turned the corner sharply and headed for the dock where the *Catalina II* was moored. He turned and squinted into the sun, trying to see who was driving. As he suspected, it was his close friend, Stan Wilson, a high-spirited Australian with plenty of experience diving the Great Barrier Reef. He would be the other diver in the water outside the cage with Mark during the shark encounters. "Nice driving, cowboy," Mark yelled into the open driver's-side window.

"Sorry we're late, mate," said Stan with his usual infectious grin. "Had to stop and pick up some shrimp for the barby."

"Oh, give me a break," groaned Mark. "Are you still trying to convince people that you're really an Aussie?" The other five team members, four crew who would operate the boat and Eric Webber, the still-photographer, just shook their heads and laughed as they got out of the van and started to load the rest of the dive equipment, listening to the usual by-play between two good friends. Mark introduced Terry to the team, but she already knew Stan from previous dives and they exchanged an affectionate hug. "Great to see you, babe," he gushed.

"Bring your Bowie knife?" Terry teased.

"Sorry, babe, that's the other Aussie, with the black cowboy hat."

By 2 o'clock that afternoon, everything was finally ready. Mark and Terry threw off the fore and aft mooring lines and headed out to the dive site, just off San Miguel Island, the westernmost of the Channel Islands, located about 55 miles off the coast. Once they arrived, Mark explained the dive plan to the team. "OK, it's pretty late in the day, so we'll just do one short dive, and we'll stay entirely inside the cage. While the cage is at the surface we'll jump into the water, swim over to it and enter through the hatch at the top. It's rigged to be just slightly negatively buoyant, so we can lower it to whatever depth we want without putting any strain on the boat's rigging. Our goals for today are to get acclimated to the conditions out here, to get used to being in the water with some big animals and to study their reactions to us. Eric will take still-photos and Terry will take video. Stan and I will be focusing on watching the swimming patterns of the sharks so we can figure out our strategy when we're outside the cage tomorrow. Check your air gauges and make sure your tanks are full at 3000psi (pounds of pressure per square inch). We'll only be 25 to 30 feet down so we should be able to stay under for at least an hour, but if anyone is cold or low on air, about 700 to 800 pounds, signal me and we all go up in the cage together. At the surface we exit from the top of the cage and swim over the to boat. Any questions?"

"What kind of sharks do you think we'll encounter?" asked Stan.

"Mostly blue sharks, but we might also see some mako, possibly a white-tip or even a great white, if we're lucky. There are lots of sea lions around and whites really love to dine on them."

"Let's hope we aren't that lucky," quipped Eric.

"We see 'em quite a bit back home," said Stan. "One of our nicknames for 'em is White Pointer."

Terry listened intently to Mark's briefing, but was apprehensively quiet.

The cage was swung out over the water and lowered. The four divers jumped into the water and quickly swam to the cage and entered. The cage was allowed to sink to a depth of 25 feet and the divers began looking around. An occasional sea lion from a nearby community swam by out of curiosity to check out the intruders inside the strange object hanging in the water. A school of tuna quickly swam by, chasing some smaller fish. Then out of the deep blue, a torpedo-like form materialized as if from nowhere, then another, and suddenly several large blue sharks, ranging from 9 to 12 feet, surrounded them.

Eric started snapping still-photos as quickly as he could frame his shots. Terry shot video, trying to pan the camera to keep each shark in the scene as long as possible. Stan and Mark watched the sharks intently, trying to gauge their speed, turning radius, frequency of turns and passes, and other information that would keep them alive outside the cage tomorrow. The sharks grew bolder and more curious, bumping the cage and occasionally mouthing the bars like a baby teething. Occasionally a tooth would fall out and drop to the wire mesh bottom of the cage, a free souvenir. This was

Terry's first time in the water so close to sharks and Mark saw that her eyes were as wide as saucers, but she fought down the urge to panic and kept shooting video. Eventually, the blue sharks grew bored, sensing that this strange, inedible object was going to keep them from the edible treats inside, and swam off; the divers watched them disappear into deep water.

Suddenly the cage was jolted and the stunned divers turned around to see a 15-foot great white trying to push its nose between the bars. Terry dropped the video camera and froze; Eric just stared at the shark and forgot to take any pictures, Stan and Mark just looked at the shark and made sure they were away from the edge of the cage and that their hands were inside, safely away from the bars. The shark was huge, although in length it was only a couple of feet longer than the largest of the blue sharks they had just seen. White sharks are imposing animals, with a broad girth that gives them a massive appearance. Why hadn't they seen it? From which point of the compass had it come? The counter-shading of sharks – darker coloration on the top to blend into the murky bottom when seen from above, and lighter coloration on the underside to blend in with the lighter surface when viewed from below – is very effective.

After a quick bump, the shark made a slow pass over the top of the cage as the divers looked up in awe. The massive shark was silhouetted against the sunlight streaming down from the surface, and its pectoral fins resembled giant wings. Terry thought, *My God, it looks like a jumbo-jet!* It made another slow pass by the cage, only about two feet away, and Terry felt a chill go through her as she saw the shark looking at her with a cold, black eye, an eye that had no emotion, no feeling, just a cold evaluation of her, not as a person but nothing more than as a piece of food. Then, it just swam off slowly and, as they all watched, the great white just seemed to de-materialize before their eyes as it blended in perfectly with the background.

After a moment Mark broke the spell with a thumbs-up sign, diver sign language indicating that they should surface. Eric pulled on the line to indicate to the boat crew that they wished to surface. The cage was raised to 15 feet and held there for a three-minute safety stop prior to coming to the surface, a common procedure which enables divers to eliminate excess nitrogen from their bodies, reducing the possibility of contracting decompression illness, known as the "bends." As soon as the hatch was unlocked, everyone swam to the boat and the enthusiastic comments and banter started.

"Did you see that?"
"I don't believe it!"
"Incredible!"
"Wow!"
"Great job, everyone!"

Although they had no video or still shots of the great white, they had sufficient photographic material of the blue sharks to study that evening after dinner. Everyone was exhausted but looking forward to the next day's diving, when Mark and Stan would be in the water with the sharks and the actual research would begin in earnest. The sleeping quarters were cramped, but Terry and Mark didn't mind squeezing into a bunk meant for one. It had been a long, tiring day, but satisfying. Mark was exhausted and fell asleep almost immediately, despite Terry's most seductive attempts to keep him awake. She looked over at him and smiled, gently brushing back a comma of hair that had fallen across his forehead. As Terry watched him sleep, she admired his features and let her mind drift, recalling the events leading up to their first meeting and the evolution of a relationship that had changed her life.

"My God, it looks like a jumbo jet!"

Photo by Paul J. Mila
© All Rights Reserved

Chapter 2

University Of California At Santa Barbara

3 Years Earlier

Terry Hunter was 21 years old, and had just graduated from the University of California at Santa Barbara with a degree in Marine Science, including a minor in Spanish. She had moved to Santa Barbara from San Mateo, California, after completing a two-year Associate's degree in Oceanography from the College of San Mateo. Terry had researched the undergraduate programs of several universities and felt that UCSB offered the best curriculum in her chosen field of study. She was satisfied in her successful undergraduate career, graduating *magna cum laude,* setting several school records as a member of the varsity swimming team and almost never being home alone on a Saturday night.

She had just broken off a relationship that had run its course shortly after graduation. Jeff, her boyfriend of six months, was nice enough, but he wanted to get married and move back to Nebraska. Terry, however, was not ready to get tied down to a permanent commitment. She had too many horizons to explore and those horizons were where the sky meets the ocean, not the grassy plains of the Midwest. The ocean was her first love, and she felt the ocean pulling her, much as the moon's gravity pulls the tides. Terry decided to stay at UCSB and had just enrolled in the graduate program in marine science. She still wasn't sure what she might finally do for a career, maybe teach or do research, possibly work for a government service, or even for a corporation if the situation involved the ocean in some related application.

Terry was fortunate that she did not have monetary concerns. Her parents had paid for college, so there were no student loans to repay and they were prepared to continue supporting her until she found a permanent career. She even had some savings squirreled away from various part-time jobs that she had taken in college in order not to be overly dependent on her parents. Terry felt that some of their financial generosity may have been due to a degree of guilt that they felt for having divorced when she was still in high school. The divorce had been bitter and Terry was deeply hurt when her parents had split. Nevertheless, both parents were supportive of her, not only financially but also emotionally. Her mother and father instilled in her a strong sense of independence and confidence, and assured her that she could succeed in whatever she attempted to do in life.

Terry was in the student cafeteria on a lunch break between classes and, as she carried her tray past the dessert section, she was absorbed in her biggest decision of the day: apple pie or Boston cream pie. She did not notice that the line had backed up at the cashier station and she bumped into the last person on the line, spilling her hot coffee onto someone's back. "YEEOW!" the person screamed in pain as the hot coffee ran down his shirt and the back of his pants. Terry stammered in embarrassment, "Oh, oh, I'm sooo sorry, let me help you; I mean, let me dry you; I mean, let me . . ."

Mark Stafford wheeled around to see who had scalded him, and Terry found herself staring into the most penetrating blue-grey eyes she had ever seen. She found herself speechless for one of the few times in her life. Mark's look of pain and annoyance quickly melted into one of bemusement as he found himself looking into the captivating green eyes of one of the most attractive women he had ever seen. It was a magical moment, two seconds actually, but it seemed an eternity to Terry. Mark, suppressing a grin with a fake frown, said, "Do you often tailgate when you drive?" The sudden humor startled Terry out of her embarrassment and in another second both were laughing about the incident. They stepped out of the cashier line and put their food trays aside as Terry tried to dry Mark's shirt and pants with a paper towel. "I don't think sitting in soggy pants helps my appetite," Mark said. "Listen, my apartment is only a couple of blocks from here, how about tagging along with me so I can change and I'll buy you lunch, my treat."

"Oh no, it was all my fault. I couldn't let you pay!"

"OK, then, it's settled – you can treat me. let's go."

"But, wait, I mean... I don't even know your name."

"Mark... Mark Stafford. And for the police accident report, your name is?"

"Terry. Terry Hunter."

"OK, Terry Hunter, let's go; I'm hungry!"

Mark held the cafeteria door open and, with a flourish, waved Terry on through. As Terry stepped past him her head was spinning over the occurrences of the past three minutes. Her thoughts were racing. *What am I doing? How did I just agree to accompany a stranger to his apartment and buy him lunch? What just happened?* When they got to Mark's apartment after a short walk, Terry said, "I'll wait down here."

"OK; be down in a sec."

When Mark came down a few minutes later, Terry had finally composed herself enough to notice Mark's features: about six foot-two; strong, athletic build; dark hair and a great smile framing those penetrating blue-grey eyes. Mark selected a nearby restaurant where the food was noticeably better than the student cafeteria. By this time the restaurant was relatively full and seating options were limited, but there was one table available for two, tucked away in a corner. "Perfect!" said Mark.

"Perfect for what?"

"Perfect for getting to know more about the person who may

have scarred me for life!"

Terry was thrown off-balance by Mark's directness, because she was usually more in control of social situations, but found herself being attracted to him. She liked strong, intelligent men, with a good sense of humor. She tired quickly of men who were indecisive, or who lacked a sharp wit. If you couldn't keep up, you were history; it was as simple as that. Mark Stafford was certainly decisive, a take-charge kind of guy, and he made her laugh. She even enjoyed the challenge of trying to regain the upper hand when he threw her a verbal curveball. As she started to tell Mark about herself she found that he was one of the easiest people to talk to that she had ever met. He had an openness about him that was disarming and Terry felt that his eyes could see into her soul.

When she finished telling Mark about herself, Terry said, "OK, mister, your turn. Talk, unless you want to have another cup of hot coffee dumped in your lap!" Mark couldn't suppress a smile and found he was enjoying her sense of humor. They were locked on each other's eyes as he told Terry about his background.

Mark was originally from Santa Barbara, California, and a year earlier had enrolled in UCSB's Department of Marine Science graduate program for Ecology, Evolution and Marine Biology, obtaining a scholarship and a position as a graduate assistant. He was also a scuba diver, with an instructor rating, and he supplemented his income as a graduate assistant by giving scuba lessons to students at a dive shop owned by his friend, Jeff Miller. He frequently went on dive trips to the Channel Islands, off Santa Barbara, to observe the abundant large-animal sea life there, mostly seals, sea lions, and, on occasion, sharks. Mark explained to Terry that he was especially fascinated by sharks and had planned to devote a major portion of his graduate studies to studying and documenting their habits, hoping to uncover some facet of their behavior that could be used in helping their conservation.

"*Their* conservation?" Terry exclaimed. "What about *our* conservation? The last thing I want is to end up as the main course for some shark's dinner."

"Oh, all that man-eater stuff is just so much Hollywood nonsense," countered Mark. "Since *JAWS* was produced back in the 1970s, humans have wiped out almost 90% of the world's shark population."

"So?"

"Well, if you wipe out a top predator, the entire balance of sea life is disrupted. Too many seals and sea lions survive, they eat too many fish and so on." Terry was impressed by Mark's knowledge and his passion for his subject.

"Yes, I do recall reading about the importance of sharks to the ecology of the ocean, but I didn't realize the score was so lopsided in favor of us. I haven't really followed the subject that closely, though. I decided to focus my studies on preserving coral reefs."

"That's an interesting area. Did you ever consider that...."

Terry and Mark talked on and on throughout the afternoon, until the waiter interrupted their conversation. "Excuse me, but we need to get this table ready for dinner." They were both stunned to discover it was almost 5:30; where had the time gone? As they were getting up to leave, Terry's mind was racing. *He never asked for my number. Will I ever see him again? Does he want to see me again?*

Once again, Mark's sense of humor resolved the situation. "Well, can I call you to let you know how my burns are healing?" he asked with a disarming grin. Terry was thrilled, but didn't dare let it show.

"What makes you think I care?" Now it was Mark's turn to be thrown off-balance – something he wasn't used to, either. As Mark was mentally groping for a response, he caught the look in Terry's eyes turn from mock indifference to a mischievous twinkle.

"Well, I just thought you were the kind of person who took responsibility for her crimes."

"Wrong!" said Terry, as she turned to walk away. Mark just stood there, dumbfounded, when she suddenly wheeled around and yelled to him, "337-3569 – I'll be home tomorrow night after 9:00!" Mark stared at Terry as she walked away, feeling that he had just met the most incredible women of his life.

Mark called Terry at 9:15 the following night and they talked until almost 11:00, agreeing to meet for lunch between classes the next day, and the next, and the next. They were becoming friends and Terry wondered why Mark had not asked her for a date yet. Most men didn't wait long to ask Terry Hunter out, but somehow this one was different. Terry liked Mark very much, and she felt a growing attraction to him.

The next Friday at lunch Mark asked Terry if she would like to have dinner Saturday. Terry was ecstatic, but said in her most serious tone, "You don't give a girl much notice do you, mister Stafford? I may be busy tomorrow; I'll have to check my calendar and get back to you." Terry saw at once in Mark's eyes that he could read her, so the game was up. They both just laughed.

Mark picked up Terry Saturday night at 8:00 and was taken aback by how beautiful she was. He already knew very well that she was an attractive woman, but had never seen her really dressed up for a date. She wore a tight-fitting, blue dress that was tastefully revealing and, as she slid into the seat next to him, Mark caught the pleasant fragrance of her perfume. It was *White Linen*, a subtle but seductive scent that Terry wore for special situations. Mark had selected a restaurant that had a dock with open-air seating by the water and they enjoyed watching a colorful sunset as they sipped champagne.

After dessert, they stepped away from the dining area over to the railing at the edge of the dock and looked out over the water. An occasional ripple broke the reflection of the full moon on the water whenever a fish jumped and broke the surface.

Neither Terry nor Mark said a word for several minutes, as each was lost in their own thoughts about where this evening was headed. Terry turned to face Mark and saw that he was looking at her. Their eyes locked on each other and suddenly Mark took Terry in his arms and kissed her, a long, lingering kiss, full on her lips. As Mark drew back momentarily, the attraction that had been building up in Terry broke through and she pulled him to her and kissed him back with fierce intensity. They embraced, kissed again and Terry felt her knees grow weak.

Between breaths Mark asked, "How about going back to my place?"

Terry said, "Can we go right now?"

They were both glad the ride back to Mark's apartment was short. As soon as they got inside they threw themselves into each other's arms. Mark was extremely intense, yet sensitive, and Terry felt herself immediately aroused to his touch. Mark responded to Terry's natural sensuality and they let their passions consume them as they reacted to each other's bodies. Sometime after midnight they fell into an exhausted embrace and slept until late morning. Terry woke up to the feeling of Mark nuzzling her ear and smiled lazily, "I think I just returned from Heaven."

"I can take you back there if you like," said Mark.

"Mmmm, maybe after breakfast."

Mark jumped out of bed to cook breakfast as Terry dozed off again and she awoke to the delicious smell of hot brewed coffee, pancakes and crispy bacon. They talked over breakfast like a married couple starting their day together. Being together just felt very natural. After breakfast they each took another cup of coffee and went out on the small balcony of Mark's apartment, facing the ocean.

"Wow, what a view," said Terry. "I had no idea last night that this view was out here." Mark stepped behind Terry, brushed her hair aside with his hand and kissed her softly on the nape of her neck. Terry shivered and smiled as she felt a pleasant tingle run through her spine. She turned to face Mark and, as she playfully nibbled his ear, whispered, "Oh, Mr. Stafford, you really know how to wake a girl up."

They sat down next to each other on a small rattan settee on the balcony and held hands as they talked. Mark said, "So, you're a record-setting swimmer, you love the ocean but have never taken scuba lessons? How come?"

"I don't know. I do like to snorkel, but I just never visualized myself being underwater."

"Well, you could certainly handle it. And you would really see the ocean that you love so much from a different perspective. It really is an amazing world, being down there among the fish, the corals and other creatures."

"Maybe you're right. It would be nice to experience everything up close instead of looking down from the surface." Mark could see that he was convincing Terry.

"The best part is that we could experience it together. I sure could use some help in my research. I think we would make a fabulous team! My friend Jeff owns *Scuba Buddies* dive shop. You could take your classroom lessons there and, since I'm a certified instructor, I could give you the pool and open water lessons. You could be certified in a couple of weeks." Visualizing diving together and sharing adventures with Mark clinched it for Terry.

"OK; let's do it!" she said decisively. Terry stepped back inside to get one last cup of coffee and, as she was pouring, felt Mark's strong arms close around her waist.

"Want another cup?" she asked.

"No," he said, kissing her again on the back of her neck, "I'm going to take us back to Heaven."

Several hours later they showered and Mark drove Terry back to her dormitory. They kissed briefly and made plans to see each other tomorrow. They were lovers as well as friends now, and that gave them a sense of direction about their relationship.

On Monday morning Terry went to Scuba Buddies. Mark had told Jeff, his friend and owner of the dive shop, about meeting someone special about a week ago and he had described Terry. Consequently, Jeff knew exactly who she was the second she walked in. *How many tall, athletic women with long auburn hair and beautiful green eyes walk into your shop everyday?* thought Jeff. "Hi, I'm Terry Hunter. You must be Jeff."

"Yes I am, nice to meet you. Mark told me you might be stopping in." Terry signed up for lessons, on the condition that Mark would be her instructor. She made an appointment to begin classes and bought her equipment: scuba mask and snorkel, open-heel fins, booties, air regulator, Buoyancy Compensating Device, also called a BC, which is an inflatable vest used to control buoyancy, a dive computer, a 3-mil thick wet suit for her pool lessons and a 7-mil thick wet suit and hood for diving in colder water, common to much of California.

Terry started her classes the next evening and was surprised by how much there was to learn about diving. "Gee, I always thought that you just kind of jump in and go down and then come up when you're low on air," she remarked to another student during a break in the class lecture on Boyle's law on gases, concerning the inverse relationship between pressure and volume. Finding out that your lungs could explode if you held your breath and did not exhale while ascending, because the decreasing pressure as you rose caused the air in your lungs to expand, really caught her attention. "OK, the number-one rule of scuba diving: *Never hold your breath; Got it!*" she said as she made a note and underlined it in her instruction manual.

Terry's lessons went well and she quickly learned the required scuba-diving skills, but not without some minor incidents. She mastered clearing a flooded mask underwater easily enough, but when she tried removing and retrieving her air regulator, she forgot to clear it first by blowing air into it or by pressing the "purge" button, before breathing. So, she inhaled water instead of air with her first breath. Luckily, this skill was first taught while kneeling on the bottom in shallow water, five feet or so. She leaped to her feet gasping for air in a gagging and coughing fit. As Terry held onto Mark to steady herself, she gasped through teary eyes, "When does it become fun, Mark?"

"Don't worry," he laughed, "Most people don't make that mistake more than once. OK, let's try it again."

Later, she moved on to other skills, learning to perform an emergency ascent without air, and simulating an out-of-air situation by taking your buddy's alternate air source, called the "octopus" regulator, and breathing from it. Finally, she learned how to equalize her ears by holding her nose and gently blowing air into the space behind the eardrum, which prevents the increasing water pressure during descent from damaging the eardrum, middle and inner ear, and, lastly, buoyancy control, in order to achieve weightlessness and to be able to hover easily at any depth in the water.

Within two weeks she completed the requirements for her basic open-water certification and Mark bought her a gold chain with a gold diver charm as a graduation present. "Always wear this," he told her, "it will bring you good luck and remind you of me whenever you go diving without me."

Terry was thrilled and as she kissed him she whispered in his ear, "I will never take it off."

Chapter 3

The Channel Islands

Present Day

The next morning everyone was ready to go by 9 o'clock, and two dives were planned for the day. By now the routine was familiar: Go over the dive plan, swing the cage over the water, jump in, swim to the cage, look for sharks. Mark presented the dive plan: "OK, for the first dive Stan and I will be outside the cage. Stan will be the guard, and Eric and Terry have photo duty. We should be in the water about an hour at a depth of 25 to 30 feet. Any questions?" By this time everyone knew their assignments and what to expect, so there were no questions. In a few minutes the cage was in the water and the divers were entering through the hatch at the top.

They did not have to wait long for the first shark to appear, a large, solitary 12-foot blue shark. Mark and Stan exited the cage and Terry and Eric took up photo stations. The shark circled the cage in a wide arc around the two divers. They were both equipped with "shark billies," three-foot long clubs studded with nails at the end. On this dive Mark would continuously face the shark and Stan would cover Mark's back in the event any other sharks swam in from Mark's blind side.

This shark was extremely cautious, maintaining a wide arc around the divers, some 40 feet away. Mark grew impatient after several minutes and decided to press the issue by swimming slowly toward the shark. When he closed to within 20 feet, he noticed the shark's swimming pattern change, from smooth and slow to quick, erratic and jerky. Then the shark raised its snout and arched its back while lowering its pectoral fins. Mark instantly recognized this body language as a reaction to what the shark perceived as a threat and a violation of its personal space, as if to communicate, *"back off or you will be attacked."* He had seen this threat behavior among grey reef sharks in the Western Pacific, but had never noticed it among blue sharks before. Mark quickly retreated back near the cage and the shark relaxed.

Then, its curiosity aroused, the shark started to close in on Mark by swimming in tighter circles. Mark rotated his body accordingly as the shark circled, in order to keep facing the animal. Suddenly the shark broke the circling pattern and slowly swam directly at Mark. This was the moment of truth, trying not to swim away but staying in position as the shark closed. As the shark drew to within five feet, Mark firmly shoved the club into its nose and the shark veered off, then circled back for another pass.

When it came in again Mark shoved the club into the side of its snout and it passed by again. One more time it came in, but Mark could perceive that it did so with a degree of uncertainty, not quite as aggressively. This time, as Mark prepared to shove the club into its face, the shark veered off before he could do so. As the shark passed, Mark gave it one more determined shove into its flank, as if to say, *"And stay away!"* The shark kept on its path and disappeared into the blue gloom from where it had come.

Mark turned to Stan, who had been watching the encounter intently, and both gave each other the three-finger circle sign, signifying, "OK!" They remained in the open water for a few more minutes and, just as they were preparing to re-enter the cage, a moving shadow caught Terry's eye and she turned to see an oceanic white-tip pass by on the other side of the cage. This was a pelagic shark, normally seen farther out in the deep ocean. She pulled out her dive knife from the sheath strapped to her calf and rapped the bars of the cage with the metallic butt-end of the knife to get Mark's and Stan's attention. They looked over and saw the shark and swam to that side of the cage. After making one wide, lazy circle, the shark swam off toward its original course, cruising on to some destination that it may have already had in mind. By this time the team had been in the water for almost an hour, so they decided to surface.

Back on the boat, they were all ecstatic about what they had just experienced. Terry had never seen Mark so animated. "Did you see the action between that sucker and me?" Mark exclaimed, as he pantomimed jabbing at an invisible shark with an imaginary club. They all had a good laugh and broke for lunch on the stern of the boat before their next dive.

While eating, they noticed a commotion in the water about a quarter of a mile off the stern. They looked over to see a large group of sea lions frantically swimming toward the shore of a distant island. Suddenly they saw the body of a large great white explode vertically out of the water, with a sea lion firmly clamped in its jaws. They watched in stunned silence as the shark fell back into the water still holding its prize; there were a few ripples, then nothing. It was over as quickly as that.

After a few moments the silence was broken by Stan, who said quietly, "Another of our nicknames for 'em back in Australia is, White Death."

The sea lions had sensed that a shark was stalking them from below and most made it to safety before the shark had taken a straggler by using a classic great white hunting technique: swimming below the chosen prey, using its counter-shading for camouflage, then, at the appropriate moment, when escape was impossible, shooting up vertically and capturing the unfortunate victim in its jaws, immediately killing or incapacitating it. No one said anything for a few seconds as they watched a red slick of blood slowly dissipate because, instinctively, each knew what the others were thinking: that a swimmer or someone paddling on a surf board would have had no chance at all against the violence of that type of attack.

"WOW!" Eric finally said. Mark knew that this hunting behavior was seen in some white shark populations but not others. Why? Was this instinct or a learned behavior? Could white sharks teach hunting techniques to their young? Not likely. Sharks do not have a reputation as doting parents. Did sharks observe and imitate the successful hunting tactics of other sharks? Mark discussed his thoughts with Terry and suggested that they tackle this as a future research project after this trip was completed.

The plan for the second dive was for Mark and Stan to reverse roles. Stan would be the "bait" and Mark would cover his back. Eric and Terry would continue to serve at photographers, remaining inside the cage. Terry had no desire to be with sharks outside the safe confines of the cage and Eric was on the team because he was a highly regarded underwater photographer, who had a definite aversion to deliberately putting himself into harm's way.

This time they had to wait almost thirty minutes for the first shark to appear. Stan moved into position, with Mark covering his flank. Everything went smoothly at first. The shark circled and Stan and Mark rotated accordingly. The shark made a pass and Stan deflected it with the shark club. It came in again... *wait; that was too soon for it to be in position to return.* Then they realized it was not one, but a pair of blue sharks. This was why the second diver was in the water. Mark moved so he was positioned back-to-back with Stan, air tanks clanking against each other. Now they could watch both sharks and visually cover a 360-degree radius.

They fended off the sharks while Terry and Eric documented the action. Now there was a problem. They had already been underwater for over 30 minutes before the sharks had appeared and Mark was running low on air, only 700psi remaining. During a momentary lull in the action he signaled Stan to check his air gauge. He was not much better off, at 900psi. If the sharks didn't leave soon they would have to break their defensive formation, making them vulnerable, then try to get back into the cage as quickly as possible.

This pair was more persistent than the single one Mark had faced earlier. *Didn't they get it?* Mark made another mental note: *next time, have spare air tanks hanging from the cage in case of this type of emergency.*

Finally, when both divers were down to 500psi, critically low, the sharks, for no apparent reason, decided to leave. Maybe they thought they were facing a new creature, with four arms and four legs – an octopus that blew bubbles? It was if the two sharks said to each other, *Hey, let's split and go find some familiar food.*

Back aboard the boat, the team shared their observations and then went below for hot showers, dinner and to review the day's action on video. Mark was confident that they had gathered sufficient data to back up his theory, that the best defense is a good offense when dealing with sharks. The team agreed that they had enough material to enable them to cut the expedition short and conclude after tomorrow's two planned dives. That was fine with Mark and Terry. They would have more time to visit with his parents. Mark's secret agenda was to spring his romantic surprise on Terry and then have his parents join them for a celebratory engagement dinner.

The final day was outstanding for diving and underwater photography: a clear, warm day with no wind and a calm sea. Mark couldn't believe how luckily this trip had turned out. Good weather and sea life had cooperated.

For this first dive Mark and Stan would reverse roles again, with Mark playing shark-bait and Stan providing cover. Once in the water a shark showed up almost immediately, another blue. *Great,* Mark thought, *we're starting immediately, so we should have no low-air problems like yesterday.*

Then, a second blue joined in and Stan went into action. Mark had no problem controlling the sharks, even when both came in on his angle. Then all of a sudden there were three sharks. This changed the equation, but not critically. Mark and Stan moved as one, rotating a little more quickly to keep all the sharks in view. Stan noticed a fourth shark circling in the distance. He reached behind him and tapped Mark on the shoulder and pointed out the newest intruder. Mark acknowledged and continued to fend off the sharks as they made pass after pass.

In the cage Terry was growing more concerned and anxious. *We have enough documentation – you proved your point, Mark, let's get the hell out of here!* She also noticed that as Mark and Stan continued to revolve around each other, they were slowly drifting farther and farther away from the cage. Initially they had been only about 20 feet away, but now they had drifted about 50 feet away. As the sharks were circling, one of the smaller blues, a four-footer, only a juvenile, cut his turn short and zeroed in on Mark's leg. Mark was momentarily distracted watching for the fourth shark in the distance and did not realize what the shark had done until he felt, not pain, but pressure seizing his right leg, just above his ankle. He looked down just as the shark shook its head, in the same manner as a dog shaking a bone. He was jerked down and, as Terry suddenly saw what was happening, she gripped the bars of the cage in terror. Mark started to pound the shark on top of its head with his club but it would not release its grip on his leg, which was now bleeding severely.

Stan noticed the movement and looked around, but did not realize what had happened until he saw a stream of blue-green fluid trailing away. Underwater, red is the first color in the spectrum to fade, so blood does not appear to be red. His eyes quickly followed the trail back to Mark's leg and he descended a few feet to get an angle on the small shark so he could rap it on its sensitive nose as it continued to thrash. The two divers were so distracted trying to fend off the small but aggressive shark, that they did not realize they had drifted another 20 feet from the cage and would have to swim back almost 70 feet against a moderate current in order to reach it.

By this time, the other three sharks had become agitated and excited by the scent of blood in the water and the thrashing of their comrade. Stan, preoccupied with beating off the shark that had fastened itself to Mark's leg, never saw the shark that sank its razor-sharp teeth into his upper left arm. He quickly rolled away and began beating this shark on the snout with his club. It soon let go, but Stan was in no position to assist Mark, having to use his right hand to hold his torn, bloody arm together as best he could as he finned hard for the safety of the cage.

Terry saw Mark struggling to swim back to the cage, still dragging the small shark along. 70 feet away, 60 feet, 50 feet, closer and closer, but agonizingly so. Finally, Terry decided she had to take action. Overcoming her own terror, she left the cage to help Mark. Terry passed Stan as she exited the cage and grabbed his shark club. She saw Mark swimming toward her, trailing a stream of blood and mangled flesh from his leg. By this time, the shark had released its grip and swam off. She swam toward Mark; less than 20 feet separated them now. Then Terry sensed a presence, felt a disturbance in the water and looked down, horrified to see a large great white rushing up from below at high speed, jaws agape. As she watched helplessly and in terror, the huge fish brushed past Terry and seized Mark by the chest, crossways in its jaws, and continued upward, breaking the surface.

The boat crew, already alerted that something was wrong by Eric frantically yanking on the emergency line to pull them up, watched in muted horror as the great white broke the surface with an already dead Mark Stafford hanging limply from its jaws, blood streaming from his severed arteries, flowing down both flanks of the shark. The beast seemed to freeze in the air for a terrible second before falling back into the water, which had turned into bloody foam. Then the shark descended back into the deep with Mark's body still in its jaws, passing only several feet from Terry, who was going into shock.

A second great white, stimulated by blood and flesh in the water, had been stalking Terry from below. In her black wet suit, her body silhouetted by the sun, Terry resembled the animal's favorite food – seal. The shark's primitive brain had completed its task of preparing for the attack, analyzing the target's speed, distance, possible threat status, and awareness of its presence: *low risk, definite food source, easy prey.* Its survival instinct satisfied, a final message was sent to its brain: *ATTACK!*

The predator turned upward toward Terry and began to increase speed. Eric, who had left the cage just behind Terry, finally caught up to her. Suddenly, the shark saw two targets, became confused, and broke off the attack to circle and re-evaluate the situation. The reprieve enabled Eric to bring Terry to the surface just as she lost consciousness. Neither had been aware of the shark's presence below them; neither of them ever realized how close to death they had been.

Back on the boat, the crew and dive team headed back to port in silence. Everyone was in various states of disbelief over what had occurred. What had seemed like an immensely successful project only several hours earlier had turned into a horrible tragedy in a matter of minutes. News of the accident had been radioed to shore and, when the research vessel and crew docked, they were met by the coast guard, police, ambulances and local news media. Stan and Terry were immediately rushed to a nearby hospital.

She was fading in and out of consciousness, but otherwise unharmed, and remained overnight for observation. Stan was fortunate that his wet suit had helped to hold his shredded arm reasonably intact with minimal loss of tissue, so the doctors were able to repair the wounds, though it required hundreds of stitches and several operations. He was devastated by the loss of his good friend.

A preliminary investigation by the local authorities, and a more detailed investigation subsequently by the university, both came to the same conclusion: that no one was to blame. It was simply a tragedy that had occurred during a high-risk project.

Chapter 4

Santa Barbara

Terry accepted the invitation of Mark's parents to stay with them until a memorial service for Mark could be arranged the following week. Mr. Stafford drove to the hospital to bring Terry to his house. When Mrs. Stafford opened the door, they both broke down briefly as they embraced. "Oh, Mrs. Stafford, I am so sorry," Terry said, sobbing.

"There, there, my dear, it wasn't your fault, so I don't want you feeling you must apologize. I know that you tried to save Mark's life."

They sat in the living room and Angela Stafford brought Terry some hot tea. Terry was inconsolable and she told Angela that she admired her strength and composure, having just lost her only son. "Well, my dear, I am sure Mr. Stafford and I will have very difficult days ahead. We are probably in a mild state of shock ourselves right now. I don't know if the reality of losing Mark has hit us yet."

After talking for a while, Angela said, "Come with me, my dear. I have something for you."

Puzzled, Terry followed Angela into the kitchen where she brought out a small jewelry box from a drawer. "At least I have two things to be thankful for," Angela Stafford said. "First, that Mark died doing something he loved, and second, that my son met you, the love of his life."

Terry was speechless and choked down a sob. "Mark asked me to hold this for him; he had planned to give it to you at the end of this trip. He meant for you to have it, so I think that you should." Terry opened the box and when she saw the round-cut diamond solitaire engagement ring, she stared at it in disbelief. The realization that the man she loved, and had been going to marry, was gone forever, and that she would never see him again, overwhelmed her. Her head started to spin and she dropped the box as she began to sink to the floor.

Suddenly, Terry felt strong, familiar arms supporting her and her head cleared enough so that she opened her eyes and found herself once again looking into the penetrating, blue-grey eyes of Mark Stafford – Mark Stafford senior.

"Oh, I am so sorry that..." but Angela Stafford cut her short, "Now there you go again, apologizing. I should have realized you wouldn't be able to handle such a shock in your fragile state right now."

"Wouldn't you prefer to keep the ring, Mrs. Stafford?"

Mr. Stafford broke in, "No, Terry, Angela and I have discussed it and Mark wanted you to have it. Our only desire is that you keep it and cherish it as a remembrance of Mark."

The next week at the memorial service, Terry was much more composed and was coming to terms with the situation, although she was still numb due to the circumstances of Mark's death. There was no body to grieve over, no final resting place to visit or over which to say a prayer or to have a private conversation. There was no closure; he was just gone. For someone who had such a strong presence in life to be just ripped from one's heart and life was somehow unsettling, unfair, bizarre. Terry left directly from the service, saying goodbye to the Staffords and to some of Mark's friends and family.

Back home, Terry felt lost around the apartment she and Mark had shared, expecting to see him come through the door at any moment, sitting in his favorite chair, lying next to her in bed. Every place she went in town she kept seeing him in her mind, remembering what they had talked about and what they had done together in almost every familiar location. This went on for the better part of a year. Her graduate studies lost their importance, and things that she had enjoyed doing with Mark gave her no more enjoyment.

Finally, Terry decided that she had to relocate in order to survive; she just had to go somewhere and rebuild her life. But doing what? Where? She still loved the ocean, despite the fact that it had taken her lover. But she felt that if she could be in the ocean she would be closer to him. Taken as he was, by a creature of the ocean, he would always be part of the ocean, in an eternal way, as part of the circle of life.

As these thoughts were running through Terry's mind, she realized she was fingering the gold diver that Mark had given her. Mark's words when he had given it to her came back to her, *"Think of me when you go diving without me."* The solution suddenly crystallized. She still loved diving, so diving would be her life. She would teach people the beauty of the undersea world, and, in the process, she would always feel close to Mark. But it would not be here; there were just too many memories. She knew she had to leave Santa Barbara, but for where?

Chapter 5

Monterey Bay, California

Mark had frequently talked to Terry about Monterey Bay, a geographical "notch" cut into the coast of central California, about three-quarters of the way north toward San Francisco. Cutting through the center of the bay was a chasm, said to be on the scale of the Grand Canyon. The "canyon" funneled an upwelling of cold water from the deep ocean, rich in nutrients. As a result, the Bay supported a broad diversity and abundance of marine life, attracting large marine animals that are normally only seen out in the deep ocean to within several hundred yards of shore. Consequently, the diving, though challenging due to rapidly changing tides, winds, visibility and currents, was extremely rewarding.

Terry had enough savings to be able to relocate, and she knew that, in a pinch, her parents would help her, although asking for their help would be a last resort. She had already completed her Master Diver certification, so the next step was instructor school. Once she was settled in an apartment, Terry immediately applied for a job at the Monterey Bay Aquarium, in order to support herself until she completed her instructor training. She had signed up for an instructor's course through a program affiliated with the National Association of Underwater Instructors (NAUI), but the next class was not scheduled to begin for about two months. She interviewed at the aquarium and was immediately hired because of her educational background and diving experience. She accepted a position as an Aquarist, a job description that covered everything from tank cleaner, specimen collector, scientist, artist, stage manager for the exhibitions, and even assistant to the veterinarian.

When the aquarium staff learned that Terry had minored in Spanish in college, and was reasonably fluent, they added another function to her job description: bilingual tour guide. The influx of Latino residents into California over the past several years had created a need for tour guides who could speak Spanish to both adult visitors and school groups. Consequently, Terry was assigned to conduct aquarium tours two mornings per week.

Terry found that, of all the functions to which she was assigned, tour guide duties gave her the most satisfaction. She enjoyed interacting with people in an educational setting because it enabled her to explain the wonders of the ocean to people who, in many cases, would not have understood or appreciated what they were looking at. She was especially attracted to the children, and enjoyed watching their eyes light up as she explained how a stingray caught its food, or how a squid could change color.

In addition to the teaching aspect of her tour-guide duties, Terry also enjoyed the way her proficiency in Spanish was improving. Her fluency had reached the point where she could answer a question immediately, without first having to translate the question from Spanish to English in her head and then translate the answer back into Spanish. Consequently, Terry asked to have her tour-guide hours increased to three mornings per week. The aquarium staff was only too happy to comply with her request, since several local schools were now requesting her by name when planning class outings to the aquarium.

Terry completed her instructor training several months later, and then applied for the job of instructor and dive master at several local dive operations. Terry was a very good diver, with excellent teaching skills, so getting hired was no problem. She could communicate technical concepts easily and effectively. Savvy dive operators knew that customers would line up for the opportunity to have a woman like Terry Hunter as their instructor, to take them diving, to just be *near* them. Within a week she had several offers. She chose Bay Divers, primarily because it was the closest dive operation to the aquarium, only a short drive away, enabling Terry to keep her position there on a part-time basis. Terry found that she could juggle both positions simultaneously, though it did not allow her to have much free time to herself. In some ways she welcomed the hectic pace, because whenever she had any free time she found herself thinking of Mark, and how much she missed him.

As the reputation of the super-attractive dive instructor at Bay Divers spread, Terry's bank account grew. She got the most customers, the biggest tips, and the most invitations to dinner. She was enjoying her success, but could not fill the void in her heart. She always wore the chain with the gold diver, and sometimes also wore Mark's diamond ring, but she found that wearing that the ring usually prompted questions about her personal life and past that she did not want to discuss.

One day she stopped by a local jeweler on her way home from work and asked the owner for some ideas on setting the diamond into something other than a ring. The jeweler, an old, kindly, sensitive gentleman knew there was always a story behind a diamond, sometimes happy, sometimes sad; he had heard them all. Terry did not mind talking to him. As she related her story, she realized it was the first time she had talked about it in over a year, and the first time ever to a total stranger. Somehow, the conversation had a cathartic effect on her and she felt better, almost as if Mark were listening.

The old jeweler noticed her gold diver and asked her if the same person who had given her the diamond ring had also given her the gold diver. Terry said yes, but she felt that the jeweler already knew the answer before she had confirmed it. "May I see it, please?" Terry lifted the chain over her head and handed it to the jeweler, who examined it carefully. "Mmmm, just as I thought."

"What is it, did you find something?"

"Well, do you see this indentation where the diver's mask is?"

"Yes, so?"

"Well, it is made that way to accommodate a stone. If you like, I could permanently set your diamond there."

"Oh, how wonderful!" Terry exclaimed. It was the solution of her dreams. As long as she wore it, Mark would always be near her heart.

"I could have it for you by tomorrow."

"OK, see you tomorrow!"

Terry slept better than she had in many months that night. She went back the next day to pick up her gold diver. When she saw how beautifully the old jeweler had set the diamond, her eyes welled up and she leaned over the counter and kissed him.

When she pulled out her wallet to pay him, the old jeweler smiled and shook his head. "It wasn't a difficult job and your appreciation is worth more than money to me."

This time Terry hugged the old man and said, "Oh, thank you, thank you. I'll never forget you!"

"Good luck, young lady, I know that one day, you will find love again." Terry smiled and waved one last time as she left the store.

Terry kept busy, working full-time at Bay Divers, and part-time at the aquarium, seeing friends and, occasionally, dating if someone captured her interest. She took each day as it came, with no long-term focus. One day, while organizing her calendar, she realized she had been working in Monterey Bay for almost three years. The change from Santa Barbara had been good for her, but Terry felt that she needed to get farther away, to get a totally fresh start, perhaps in another country. With her experience as a bilingual tour guide at the Monterey Bay Aquarium and her fluency in Spanish, Latin America would be a logical possibility, she reasoned. So, one day over lunch with some of her friends on the Bay Divers staff, she pulled out a map of Central and South America.

The U.S., Central & South America, Bordering the Caribbean

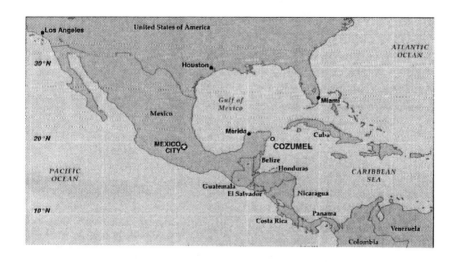

Source: *Diving & Snorkeling Cozumel,* 3rd edition, July 1998. Lonely Planet Publications

Chapter 6

Cozumel, Mexico

There are no modern jet-ways leading from the plane to the passenger terminal at Cozumel International Airport, so the steamy tropical heat felt like an oven to Terry as she stepped onto the open stairway leading down from the air-conditioned plane to the hot tarmac.

Cozumel is an island located about twelve miles from the Mexican mainland, just east of the Yucatan Peninsula, and about fifty miles south of Cancun. It lies at the northern tip of an extensive reef chain, which extends down into Central America, making it one of the longest reef systems in the world, second only to Australia's Great Barrier Reef. The island is almost thirty five miles in length, creating a channel between it and the mainland that is protected from the strong waves of the Caribbean Sea.

Most of the diving there takes place on the numerous reefs located in this channel, although some more adventurous divers occasionally brave the strong currents of the wave-battered eastern coast. A steady current flows continuously through the channel, providing a generous supply of nutrients, which is responsible for the abundant, diverse marine life and clear water, which have given Cozumel a well-deserved reputation for world-class diving. It was this reputation that attracted Terry, as she considered her options in choosing a place to build a new life.

After clearing Mexican Immigration and Customs at the airport, Terry called Hector Suarez, a friend of one of the divers at Bay Divers back in Monterey Bay. Hector had agreed to help Terry as a favor to his friend in the States, and he had a room that Terry could rent temporarily until she was settled. Hector Suarez blinked twice when he opened the door to one of most beautiful women he had ever seen.

"Hola, Hector, I am Terry Hunter," she said using her best Spanish.

"Please come in, senorita Terry" was all Hector could manage, further surprised that this American woman was also fluent in his language. "May I offer you some lunch?"

"Great, thank you. I am famished; it was a long flight," Terry said, accepting his hospitality.

After lunch, Terry went to her room and freshened up. Her next stop was to the Office of Immigration to apply for a work permit and resident status. She quickly learned during her meeting with an immigration officer that obtaining permission to stay and work in Mexico was not as easy as she had anticipated. First, she would have to find someone who would hire her. Then, her prospective boss would have to sponsor her and petition Mexican Immigration to allow her to stay in the country. After absorbing this information, Terry said to the officer, in her best Spanish and most upbeat fashion, "Well, I guess I better start looking for an employer, pronto!"

"One more thing, senorita Hunter," said the officer. "Your prospective employer cannot hire you unless he can first demonstrate that there is no qualified Mexican who can perform the same job." With this last piece of information Terry's eyes glazed over as she thought to herself, *Well, Toto, you're not in Kansas anymore!* As she got up to leave, the immigration officer wished her good luck and she flashed a smile that portrayed much more confidence than she felt at that moment.

The cab driver took a route through San Miguel that ran along the water and Terry began to feel upbeat as she watched several dive boats heading out to the reefs and saw one of the many cruise ships that visit Cozumel docking at the main pier. By the time the cab reached Hector's building, Terry's natural optimism had restored her confidence that she would find employment in one of the many dive shops on the island. Terry returned to her room and opened up a list of dive shops in Cozumel that she had cut out from various dive magazines. Cozumel was, after all, known as the "Diver's Paradise."

Hector volunteered to show Terry around the island, but it had been a busy day and she was exhausted. "Tomorrow would be much better, if you don't mind, Hector. I'd just like to read a bit, have a light dinner and hit the sack, I'm bushed."

Hector spent the next day showing Terry where the best places were to buy food and clothes, where she should shop for a car, and where the most reasonable locations were to look for her own apartment. The following morning, Terry rented a car and, with map and list of dive operators in hand, went job hunting. She decided to try near town first, reasoning that she would have the best opportunity where there was the highest concentration of dive shops. The first couple of dive operations needed no help, as they were fully staffed. At several others she was met with outright resistance, especially because she was a woman trying to break into a male-dominated culture.

"Well, that's enough rejection for one day," Terry said out loud to herself. As tough and as upbeat as she was, Terry was not used to being rejected. The fact that she was in a foreign country with a limited amount of financial resources, no friends and only a few acquaintances, left Terry's confidence somewhat shaken. When she returned to Hector's apartment, he asked, "Any luck today?"

"Nope, nothing, nada," Terry said, dejectedly. Sensing her mood, Hector said "OK, pretty lady, you need to get out tonight and not think of what happened today. Isn't there a saying in your country, 'Tomorrow is another day,' from that movie, 'Going With the Breeze' or something like that?" Hector's good-natured attempt to buoy her spirits had Terry was laughing so hard that she could not contain herself.

"Sure, Hector, what the hell!" Hector couldn't understand what the joke was, but thought, *See how her eyes sparkle when she laughs!*

"Great, then we will go to one of my favorite places, Pancho's Backyard. It is close by, right in town. I will invite some of my friends and before the night is over you will have many friends in Cozumel." Terry was appreciative of Hector's efforts to cheer her up and his enthusiasm was infectious. She couldn't wait to go out and have some fun. It was only a five-minute drive to Pancho's Backyard, a restaurant located at the north end of town, just past the main tourist drag.

The restaurant was situated behind a souvenir shop and, as they walked through the shop, Terry thought, *Oh no, is he taking me to some tourist trap?* On the contrary, passing through the shop led them to a garden-like setting with low lighting and tables separated by expertly planted vegetation. Soft Mexican music played in the background. They were shown to a table where several couples were already seated. Hector proudly announced with a flourish, "These are my friends. Everyone, this is senorita Terry, from the USA, who is making her new home here with us here in Cozumel!"

"If you are Hector's friend, you are our friend, also!" one of them said. Everyone was warm and friendly and intensely curious about Terry. In a male-dominated culture it seemed so bold for a woman to leave her native country and begin a new life, especially a women who was alone. They were also fascinated by Terry's appearance. The norm among the local population was to be short and dark, so this tall, fair woman seemed all the more different and somehow mysterious. The men admired her natural beauty, though they were careful not to let their interest show in front of their female companions. Terry's light-olive complexion, already tanned by the California sun, was several shades darker after only a few days under the more intense Cozumel sun, setting off her auburn hair and green eyes even more.

The food at Pancho's was excellent and, during a delicious seafood dinner punctuated by several rounds of margaritas, the conversation got around to Terry's future plans and her disappointing experience earlier that day. One of Hector's friends suggested that she try her luck farther out, south from town, where the dive operations were more closely tied to the large luxury hotels. "Yes," said another, "One of the busiest and best is Playa Divers, next to the Palancar Princess. I know the owner, Oscar. He is a little strange, but they are so busy that they always need help, and the tips are good, too."

"Thanks, can I use your name as a reference?"

"Of course, pretty lady. Just tell Oscar that Raul Pagan sent you."

"Great! That's where I'll be tomorrow!" As the group got up to leave, Terry felt a thousand times better than she had only a couple of hours earlier. She had been treated to a great meal, met some wonderful new friends, and had a line on a possible job. *What more could a girl ask for,* she thought.

The next morning she drove to the Palancar Princess hotel in her rented car and parked in the guest parking lot. "Excuse me, senor, where can I find Playa Divers dive shop?"

The guard pointed her in a direction toward the beach. "You will see the sign for the dive shop from there, senorita."

Terry walked toward the beach and was impressed by the expanse of beautiful sand, punctuated by palm grass umbrellas and palm trees bordering the edge of the water. The dive shop was located about a hundred yards down the beach next to a pier where the dive boats were moored. Terry walked along the water's edge, enjoying the feeling of the tropical 80-degree water as she splashed along.

She went into the dive shop and asked for Oscar. The cashier behind the counter eyed her suspiciously, which made Terry wonder how many women came in asking to see Oscar, *and,* she also wondered, *what for?*

The cashier said, "Wait here a minute" in an annoyed tone. A couple of minutes later, a short, stocky man, about 5'6," 185 pounds, with shiny black hair combed straight back, about 45 years old, came out. "Who wants to see me?" he asked, more as a challenge that a question.

"Hola, senor, my name is Terry Hunter," she said, extending her hand, "I recently moved to Cozumel and I am looking for a job. Raul Pagan said you might be able to help me."

Oscar blinked twice, not expecting to meet such a beautiful woman today. He extended his hand as an afterthought, not used to such a forward approach from a woman.

"I already have a cashier. I have people to give out equipment and sell the dive trips. I don't need any help."

"I'm a dive instructor and I am looking to get a position teaching or as a dive master."

Oscar thought for a minute. He had just lost a dive instructor to a competitor and his busy season was fast approaching. *But hire a woman?* His mind was racing, wondering if he should offer her a job or proposition her. "What is your certification, PADI or NAUI?"

"I have been a NAUI instructor for over three years, and I am fluent in Spanish as well as English."

"Come into my office," he motioned with his hand to follow him. He knew that bilingual instructors were good for business. They made the customers more relaxed, more willing to spend money. "If you work for me, you work hard; no special favors because you are a woman. You carry equipment like everyone else, you dive like everyone else, put in the extra time like everyone else."

"No problem. I'm used to hard work"

"OK, I have one opening for an instructor. Be back here tomorrow at 8am sharp, bring your passport and any immigration papers you have. I have to file papers to sponsor you and then prove to the authorities that I cannot find a Mexican female dive instructor who speaks fluent English."

"Thank you very much, Mr...."

"Oscar, just Oscar. You just make sure I am not going through all this extra work for nothing."

"Thank you Oscar, you won't be disappointed," Terry said, standing up first and, once again, extending her hand first.

Oscar was not used to a woman taking this kind of initiative. It made him uncomfortable, as if he were being challenged. He extended his hand and noted her strong grip. *This is a different kind of woman*, Oscar thought to himself. Terry noted his limp handshake; *feels like I'm holding a dead fish*, she thought to herself. Terry left, retracing her route back to her car, feeling like she was walking *on* the water not *through* it.

When Hector came back to the apartment after work, Terry ran over and hugged him, kissing him on the cheek. "I got the job!" she exclaimed, "I owe it all to you and Raul! First paycheck, dinner is on me!"

It took a while for Terry to be accepted by the rest of the Playa Divers staff, but they soon saw that she worked as hard as they did, was a good instructor and was a very good diver. After a while they treated her as one of the team, inviting her to parties, playing the same practical jokes on her as on each other, and depending on her in difficult dive situations.

One day, on a large group dive, Terry served as a second dive master so the group could be split into two, smaller, more manageable groups. At 60 feet the other dive master didn't realize that one of the divers in his group was having trouble breathing, not getting sufficient air from his regulator, starting to panic, and his dive buddy was too inexperienced to help. Terry noticed at once, swimming over in front of him and squeezing his arm so hard that the sudden pain made him focus on her. She then held the mouthpiece from her emergency "octopus" regulator directly in front of the diver's facemask and, as she had hoped, he understood what to do. He took out the mouthpiece from his malfunctioning regulator and replaced it with Terry's. She maintained her hold on him until he cleared the regulator of water and began to breath normally, then escorted him to the surface in a slow, controlled ascent. The dive staff knew that she had probably saved the diver's life, along with the reputation of Playa Divers. The fact that she didn't gloat or hold it over the other dive master was not lost on the staff. She was now accepted, really, "one of the guys."

Except for Oscar. Terry could sense that, for some reason, he did not like her. He went out of his way to make things just a little more difficult for her and occasionally she caught him out of the corner of her eye, leering at her in a way that unnerved her. Terry decided to handle the situation by ignoring Oscar and avoiding him as much as possible. He interpreted her behavior as being disrespectful, which infuriated him even more. Oscar fancied himself a great lover, someone to whom any woman should show immense gratitude just to be shown the least bit of attention by him. Consequently, Terry's aloofness was a direct affront to his inflated, macho self-image. Oscar vowed to himself that one day he would teach Miss Terry Hunter, the tall American beauty, some humility, as well as respect.

Chapter 7

New York City, Lower Manhattan

Eddie Connors stood on the corner of Wall and Broad in the financial district of New York City, checking the time on his new Seiko. *Almost 5:30, where is she?* he was wondering, as nearby office buildings began to empty out and a surge of humanity started to rush by in a hurry to begin another summer weekend.

Looking down Wall Street, he spotted a hand waving above a wind-blown head of blonde hair, about a block away. He smiled in recognition and waved back. "Sorry, I'm late, hon," said his girlfriend, Lauren Blake, giving him a light peck on the lips. "Had to retype an important letter for my anal boss for the fifth time so he could get it out tonight. He kept changing the damn thing every time he proofed it."

"No problem, babe," said Eddie as they locked arms and walked toward the Broad Street subway station. "One quick stop first. Gotta see Charlie D and get our stuff." As he said the name, Eddie briefly wondered what the "D" stood for. Was it the initial of Charlie's last name, or related to some other moniker? He met Charlie D about a year ago, but did not know very much about him, other than his name and line of business. *Oh well, who cares?*

They stopped at a newsstand near the subway entrance and Eddie said, "Hey, Charlie, how's it goin'? Gimme the usual." Charlie D reached under the counter and pulled out a folded *New York Post* and handed it to Eddie. Eddie gave Charlie a fifty-dollar bill, tucked the newspaper tightly under his arm and he and Lauren headed down the stairs to the crowded platform.

Anyone paying attention to the transaction would have thought it odd that Eddie never received any change, but, then again, in New York City no one really looks at anyone long enough to notice much of anything about someone else's business – especially at rush hour. In fact, legend has it that a middle-aged gentleman suffered a fatal heart attack one evening while standing, packed shoulder-to-shoulder, back-to-back among fellow strap-hangers in a crowded subway car. No one noticed what had happened to the unfortunate fellow until the crowd thinned out a bit at a station, and he collapsed, since there were no other bodies to support him. It was supposedly reported that the passengers did step over him carefully, however, as they quickly headed for their connecting trains and other destinations.

Eddie and Lauren caught the "R" train, to Bay Ridge, Brooklyn, where they lived in a small, but well kept, apartment. They stood for most of the forty-minute ride, and then it was only a five-minute walk from the 69th Street station to their apartment. Once inside, Eddie collapsed onto the sofa while Lauren checked to see if Ginger, their two-year old cat, had finished her food. "What a week," he said. "Buried under a ton of paperwork that never lets up. I hate this crummy job!" Lauren came inside and sat next to him, nuzzling his ear playfully.

"Well, we have two days not to think about our jobs, so let's make the most of it." They were both marginally employed. He, in a back-office operations job at one of the few mid-sized banks that had managed to avoid getting swallowed up by the major financial institutions; she, a junior-level administrative assistant at a brokerage firm. They were high-school sweethearts who had wanted to start fast in life. So they bypassed college and obtained entry-level jobs right out of school.

Now, however, they were just beginning to realize that what had seemed like good money at first would not carry them very far, certainly not very far past their cozy apartment in Brooklyn. They could not afford to go away on vacation very often, but they could afford some other minor luxuries – like an occasional hit of cocaine on weekends. It made them feel good, enabling them to temporarily forget about their limited prospects.

"Hey, whad-ya get from Charlie D?" asked Lauren. Eddie unfolded the newspaper, inside of which was taped a small brown bag that contained their weekend enjoyment.

"Wanna have a little jolt before dinner?" he asked.

"Sure, I could use a little lift." Eddie spread some of the cocaine onto a small, smooth, glass table, then took a razor blade and deftly cut a line of coke for each of them. Lauren got two small straws, handed one to Eddie, and they both ingested the drug by snorting it into one nostril while squeezing the other shut. Then, they both leaned back, relaxed and waited for the magic powder to do its work. After a few minutes, Eddie felt a strange, unfamiliar sensation in his chest, a strong, fluttering feeling. He loosened his shirt. Lauren blinked her eyes a couple of times and shook her head, trying to clear a strange, fuzzy feeling.

"Hey, babe, I don't feel so good," Eddie said, holding his chest as the fluttering in his chest became a more pronounced pounding. *Holy shit, this really feels bad!*

"Hon, I can't catch my breath," was the last thing that Eddie was able to hear Lauren say, as he passed out when his heart went into a deadly, uncontrolled fibrillation and his blood pressure plummeted. Lauren tried to stand up and get to the bathroom, but fainted from lack of oxygen as she went into respiratory arrest. She lay on the floor next to Eddie for several minutes, her body reflexively heaving, vainly trying to get air. Then, Lauren's pallor began turning a sickly, pale shade of blue and her vital organs began to shut down.

Ginger, startled out of a catnap by the sound of Lauren falling to the floor, curiously entered the room to investigate. She sniffed Lauren, looked into her sightless eyes, and then her back arched and fur stood on end, as her instinct sent a message to her brain that something was terribly wrong. She fled the room.

Chapter 8

Cozumel

One Year Later

Terry had spent the year working hard for Playa Divers, instructing new divers who were in the process of becoming certified or trying out scuba for the first time, serving as a dive master for a group of already-certified divers, even being assigned as the personal dive guide for visiting VIPs – whatever was necessary. She was usually the first one in the dive shop in the morning, personally checking the equipment that she and her divers would use that day, being available to spend time with her customers before a dive, to chat and get to know them. She learned, even before the first fin touched water that day, which divers would require more of her attention on a dive because they were less skilled and prone to anxiety,

49

and which ones were more advanced and self-sufficient. Consequently, she had fewer emergency situations and more successful dives than most of the other dive masters.

She also dove frequently on her own time, as well, to familiarize herself with the ecology of the various reefs. Many fish and sea creatures are territorial, tending to live their lives on a particular reef where they have found shelter safe from predators and a good food supply. Other members of the undersea community tend to be transient, visiting various reefs that appeal to them for one reason or another, avoiding others, and looking for food in open water or in the sandy areas separating the reefs. Terry learned who lived where, and who was likely to show up at various locations. Consequently, when divers had special requests, like, "Hey, we'd like to find a sea horse," or, "Can we see a turtle and a nurse shark today?" she knew where to look.

There were no guarantees, of course, but her knowledge of the area improved the odds for success in granting her customers' requests, which also improved the tips that she received and resulted in return business for Playa Divers.

Terry was happy, saving some money, furnishing her modest apartment, and otherwise getting her life in order in her newly adopted country. Late one afternoon, she returned to the Playa Divers office after the day's diving to complete some paperwork. It had been an unusually busy day, with two-tank dives both in the morning and afternoon. Four dives in one day was a hard day's work, especially since the current had been stronger than usual that day.

As she was getting ready to leave, Oscar came by and said, "Terry, I need you to come back to the office after you get some dinner, to run a classroom session with some divers taking their certification course."

This was the last thing Terry needed after a long day, but she and Oscar had been getting along worse than usual lately and she didn't want to give him any cause to make her life more difficult.

"OK, Oscar. I'll be back by 6:30. Can we do it then?"

"No, I scheduled it for 8:00; don't come before then!" *Shit,* thought Terry, *there he goes again, being more difficult just to bust my chops.*

50

"Fine, see you then," Terry said as she walked out brusquely without looking back. As she left, Oscar glared at her for, once again, not showing him the proper respect he felt he deserved.

When Terry returned later that evening, she searched for the dive students she was supposed to teach but the office was deserted. She heard the office door slam behind her and she turned to find herself face-to-face with a very inebriated Oscar. She immediately put it all together, realizing that she had been set up, and tried to leave. As she tried to step around Oscar he grabbed her by the shoulders and pushed her down on the couch in the office. She started to get up but he slapped her hard across the face and she fell back on the couch.

"American bitch! I will teach you some respect. Tonight you will find out what a real man is like!" As Terry tried to clear her head, Oscar was suddenly on her.

She struggled, but he was too heavy and, as he proceeded to grind his pelvis against her, she felt his erection. Terry panicked as she realized what was coming next. He tried to kiss her, but she kept rapidly tossing her head left and right to keep away from his mouth and stinking breath. Finally, he grabbed her hair and held her head still as he tried to tongue her, but her chain with the gold diver kept getting in the way. Oscar ripped it off her neck with his other hand and threw it across the room, yelling, "Get this cheap piece of trash off!" The sharp pain of the chain being torn from Terry's neck, and Oscar's desecration of her late-lover's gift, her most cherished possession, jolted Terry into a fierce rage. She drew her right leg up so that her knee was between her chest and Oscar's and then, gathering all her strength, she kicked as hard as she could.

The blow struck Oscar off-center, throwing him off the couch onto the floor, on his back. The shock of landing on the floor stunned Oscar momentarily. He started to get up, but Terry had already jumped to her feet and had grabbed the nearest object she could find – a ceramic lamp – and rammed it into Oscar's head, smashing the lamp into hundreds of shards, lacerating his forehead and scalp. He fell back again and, before he could get up, a hard, well-placed kick to his testicles ended his plans for the evening. Erection over. Oscar doubled over into a fetal position, howling in pain.

Suddenly, he felt his head being jerked up as Terry grabbed him by the hair. He looked up through a bloody fog, but all he could focus on were Terry's blazing green eyes. Oscar had never seen such rage and hatred in the eyes of any living creature before, on the land or sea.

"You fucking bastard. If you ever touch me again, if you ever come near me again, I'll kill you! Comprende?"

All Oscar could do was grunt an acknowledgment and then Terry slammed his face into the floor, bloodying his nose. She walked over to the other side of the room to retrieve her chain and gold diver, and the last thing a very dazed Oscar heard before the door slammed was Terry's final comment as she stormed out of the office. "Filthy son-of-a-bitch!"

The next day Terry arrived for work as usual. She knew her days working at Playa Divers were numbered, but she couldn't afford to just quit. As she was going about her business of preparing for the day's diving, there was an unusual buzz of animated conversation, which suddenly ceased. She looked up and saw why. Oscar had come out of his office and was standing in front of the equipment rental station. His forehead was bandaged and bruised, his nose was swollen, his right nostril filled with cotton packing, and he walked with a noticeable limp, feet slightly apart more than normal.

From the smirks and hushed comments of the dive staff, Terry guessed that Oscar must have been bragging about what he had planned to do last evening, and the staff had correctly figured out that the night had not turned out as he had planned. As Terry and Oscar looked at each other, their eyes locked and all Terry could see in his eyes was cold, malevolent hatred. She realized at that moment that she had to accelerate her plans to leave Playa Divers as quickly as possible.

That night, she asked Hector to invite Raul over for dinner. She told them what had happened and Raul suggested some other dive operators to Terry. Over the next week after work she visited several dive operators who, Raul thought, could use someone like Terry. But Oscar knew many people on Cozumel, some friends and also even more people who feared to cross him. Terry soon realized that she was being blackballed.

In the meantime, Oscar made Terry's daily existence at Playa Divers hell. He knew she couldn't afford to leave and he had made it impossible

52

for her to find other work. He, Oscar, would show this bitch just who was the boss. He assigned her the longest hours, the smallest of the dive boats, doing everything he could to ensure that she received the fewest customers and the smallest tips.

Discussing the situation with Hector one evening, Terry vowed that she would not be beaten. She would start her own dive company. Hector explained that it was not that easy. First, she would have to apply to Mexican Immigration for independent status, enabling her to work as an independent contractor, on her own. Not being a Mexican citizen made this difficult, but not impossible. Hector knew a lawyer who owed him a favor. Terry and Hector paid him a visit the next day and filed the necessary papers.

Next, Terry knew that she would have to have a dive boat. Purchasing a boat was out of the question: too expensive. Raul introduced her to Manuel Lopez, an experienced captain, owner of the dive boat *Dorado*. Manuel made his living by temporarily leasing his boat to other dive operators when they needed extra capacity, usually during peak season. Terry suggested making a long-term arrangement with her, to their mutual benefit. By renting her his boat and serving as captain he would get steady income, and she would gain access to a good dive boat at a reasonable cost.

Manuel looked at Terry, admiring her beauty, and said, "Why don't you come over to my house this evening and we can discuss terms?"

Terry was apprehensive about such a meeting, but she was desperate. "All right, give me directions and I'll meet you at 8:00."

Terry went to Manuel's house at the agreed-upon time. He opened the door and ushered her into the dining area, where he had a bottle of wine and two glasses on the table. They discussed terms and, just when Terry thought they had an agreement, Manuel put his hand on Terry's. She stiffened as he said, "Before I agree to our partnership there is a special favor I would like from you."

When Terry left Manuel's apartment later that evening, she had her deal, so now she had a boat. *DiveWithTerry* was close to becoming a reality, but she knew that she still had one major hurdle to overcome.

Chapter 9

Late one afternoon, after a long, arduous day of diving, Terry told Oscar that she needed to speak with him. Oscar ushered her into his office, relishing the anticipation of watching her grovel, expecting her to plead with him to let her work fewer hours, work on a bigger boat to enable her to get better tips, *something*. When Terry told him she was leaving Playa Divers, Oscar went berserk. He hated her, but had wanted to keep her there until he could figure out a way to break her spirit. He also did not want to lose the additional revenue that he knew she was bringing in.

"You will never work anywhere else on this island," he roared. "I'm still your sponsor, you fool! One call from me to the immigration authorities telling them that I refuse to sponsor you because I say you are unfit to be here and you'll be deported!" The idea that Terry, or any woman, would ever try to strike out on her own was out of the realm of his consciousness.

Terry's petition for independent contractor status was still in process, however, so Oscar's threat put her in real jeopardy. Oscar's tirade finally unleashed Terry's own anger, which had been building up after the abuse that Oscar had put her through.

"How dare you try to stop me from having my own life?" she screamed as her eyes blazed and she took a step toward him. Her fury reminded Oscar of his recent painful incident and, reflexively, he moved a hand over his crotch. "If you ever make that call to Immigration *I'll* make a call to the police and have you arrested for attempted rape!"

Oscar was not used to such a verbal counter-attack and he blinked in surprise. The usual response to his rage, especially from a lowly employee, was cowering and subservience, but he quickly gathered himself.

"Ha! And what do you think will happen?" he said, sneering derisively. "Do you think I would ever be convicted or even be arrested? After an investigation, who will they believe? Me, a respected citizen, or a foreign bitch like you?" He took a step toward Terry but she suppressed her defensive instinct to step back and held her ground, so their eyes were glaring, inches from each other.

Terry's mind raced; the ball was in her court, but she realized that Oscar was right. She could go to the police but she was playing against the house and the deck was stacked. What was it that her father had once taught her? *When the deck is stacked, change the game.* An idea came to her. Hopefully, Oscar's own ego would be the ace up her sleeve, her own trump card.

"You may be right, Oscar. You probably have connections with the cops and half of Cozumel. Even if they investigated, you probably wouldn't even be arrested. But I bet a lot of people, your amigos as well as the people who hate your guts, will get a kick of learning why it was only *attempted* rape and not a completed rape. Maybe we can demonstrate for them how I kicked your balls through your throat and smashed your ugly face into the floor! By the way, has anyone told lately that you need a nose job?"

Terry noticed Oscar's jaw muscles clench with rage as he closed his fists and, as she saw the veins in his neck bulging with a surge of blood, she hoped she had not overplayed her hand. Every muscle in his body was tensed and ready to spring. She realized that fighting with an enraged, sober Oscar would be far more difficult than with a drunk Oscar. His eyes burned with rage, but just when Terry thought he would lunge at her she saw something flicker in his eyes, from glaring hate to a faraway look. It was if Oscar were viewing a filmstrip of how this might play out, visualizing the derision from his enemies and business associates – he had no real friends – at the public disclosure of Terry's neutralization of his manhood.

It took only a couple of seconds for Oscar to calculate his best option. "Get the fuck out of my sight before I kill you," was all he said, but in such a determined, cold, quiet tone that Terry felt a chill run down her spine and she knew that she should leave – *right now!* She turned on her heels and walked out without looking back.

Two weeks after Terry's final confrontation with Oscar, her petition for independent contractor status was granted and she focused the next several months on building her business. Fortunately for her, even though there were many people either in debt to Oscar or just too afraid to cross him, there were also even more who were happy to quietly refer extra customers to her when they were over-booked. This gave her a start.

In addition, Terry had kept an email list of her customers at Playa Divers and stayed in touch with them. Their loyalty was to her, not to Playa Divers. Consequently, when they made future dive plans they contacted her directly.

When Oscar realized *DiveWithTerry* was not only in operation but also cutting into his business, he was furious. He would figure out a way to destroy her, once and for all.

Chapter 10

New York City

Detective-Sergeant Joseph Manetta – 32 years old, nine year veteran of the New York City Police Department, currently in the Narcotics Division – walked over to the one-way window of the interview room to watch his partner, Detective Bill Ryan, interviewing a suspect they had "invited" in for a chat. Joe Manetta smiled at the sign on the door, *Interview Room*. Suspects early in an investigation were invited to come in for a friendly "interview." After there was more evidence, the next time they came in the sign on the door said, *Interrogation Room*; then, they were interrogated. *Oh well*, Joe thought, *that's what happens when you hire college guys with marketing and psychology degrees.* Joe was also a college graduate, with a degree in criminal justice from St. John's University in New York, but those marketing and psych guys always amused him.

This investigation had been frustrating and they were not much closer to tracking down the latest flow of high-grade cocaine than when had they had started over a year ago. Detectives Manetta and Ryan had been to the morgue too many times recently to attend too many autopsies of young people whose lives had been cut short by this latest flow – no, it was more like a flood – of cocaine that was not only powerful, but, for some reason, unusually deadly. As a result they were frustrated, tired, worn out, on edge.

They decided to debrief on the results of the interview over dinner and then knock off for the night. They drove downtown, to have a late dinner at a small Italian restaurant in Little Italy, which was getting more "Little" each year as Chinatown continued to grow, absorbing the Italian section building by building. At a quiet table in the corner, Joe asked his partner, "Well, are we any closer?"

"Nah, this guy was just a bottom feeder, he didn't know enough to help us or get anyone important into trouble. Besides, we didn't have much on him, only a scent on his shoes that one of our dogs picked up on. He had 101 alibis as to where it could have come from, so we let him go."

"Too bad. We gotta get lucky soon. Too many kids are ending up on a slab downtown, and now it's in all the boroughs."

"Yeah, that's what's making it so tough to trace."

After a glass of chianti, hot antipasto, veal scaloppini with angel hair pasta, tortoni and espresso, the two detectives were ready to call it a night. Bill drove to the Battery Tunnel and then out to Brooklyn. Joe followed the same route, but continued east on the Belt Parkway toward Merrick, a town on the south shore of Long Island. It was almost midnight when he pulled into the driveway.

Unlocking the front door, Joe entered an all-too-quiet house, a house that had not been so quiet only three years ago. He went into the bedroom and got undressed, hanging his 9mm automatic, still in its shoulder holster, on a chair next to the bed in the event he needed it in a hurry. No need to store it safely away from the kids; there were no kids here any more.

As he set the alarm for 6:00am, he looked at the pictures on the dresser of the bedroom set that he and his wife, Jenny, had picked out after they had gotten engaged. They had been college sweethearts and they both knew, even before graduation, that they were meant to be together forever. Joe looked at their wedding picture and thought back to when he had assumed that "forever" meant a long time. He took one of the pictures of his family in his hands and just looked at it, and just thought to himself, *senseless, so senseless.*

The accident three years ago that had claimed the lives of his twin boys, Bobby and Andy, and his wife, three months pregnant, *was* senseless. A couple of twenty-something kids, young adults really, high on drugs one Saturday night, had gotten onto the Southern State Parkway, an east-west highway running along Long Island's south shore. They were so stoned that they entered the highway on the exit ramp, ignoring the "WRONG WAY" signs and not noticing that the directional arrows embedded in the pavement were pointing against them.

With little traffic on the highway at three in the morning, they never realized they were headed west in the eastbound lane until they saw the headlights of Jenny's Honda Accord coming at them on a curve. Neither Jenny nor the sleeping children had a chance as they were crushed head-on by the Ford Explorer at a combined closing speed of over 120 miles per hour. The un-belted occupants of the Explorer didn't have much of a chance, either, as their large SUV climbed over the top of the Honda and then kept rolling over until it smashed into a tree on the shoulder of the road, spilling them out onto the highway over a distance of several hundred yards.

A couple of hours later when the police came to his house, Joe answered the door thinking maybe he was late for work or that he was being picked up for special detail, but then it registered that the uniforms in front of him were not NYPD, but Nassau County Police. That was the beginning of his nightmares, ones that he kept having all too often since that dreadful morning.

Shortly afterward, he had requested a transfer from the rackets division into the narcotics division, in an effort to try and keep tragedies such as this from happening to other families. Putting the picture back on

61

the dresser, Joe fell into bed and, after saying a prayer for his dead family, said one more prayer for himself, that he would not have another nightmare tonight.

The next morning at work, Joe got a phone call from a toxicologist working on one of the drug-related autopsies. He called Bill Ryan to the phone and put it on speaker. "What's up, Jack?"

"Some strange results, guys." Jack Phillips, chief doctor of the lab, continued, "The last two victims died from inhaling glue fumes, although the coke in their systems was a contributing factor."

"What?" said Joe, "Glue? Coke-heads don't sniff glue!"

"Yeah, I concur, but that's what the tests show."

"Can you run them again?"

"Already ran 'em twice."

"OK, thanks, Jack."

"Sorry to throw more confusion at you; call me if you have any more questions, fellas."

"We haven't seen any serious glue-sniffing here for years," said Bill, "That fell off after strict laws stopped kids from buying tubes of airplane glue at the local hobby shop to repair non-existent model airplanes."

"Yeah; besides, if you can afford to buy coke you don't use glue; and if all you can afford to buy is glue, you don't use coke. Nah, it just doesn't add up. Hey, I have an idea. Come with me." Bill and Joe went to the Property Clerk's office, where cocaine from drug busts as well as the samples found in the pockets of some of the recent victims was secured.

Joe signed out several samples of cocaine and called the chemical analysis lab. "Hello, Detective Manetta here. Listen, I know you ran tests on that coke we brought in to determine purity, but I'd like to get one more test done. We'll bring a sample right over."

At the chemical analysis lab Joe met with Sara Flynn, a friend of several years. "Sara, I know you ran the usual tests on this stuff for the us, but I'd like you to run one more test."

"OK, glad to help a friend in need. What do I look for?"

"Glue."

"Glue?"

"Yep, glue. I don't know what kind, but something that could be easily inhaled, possibly with fatal results."

The next morning the phone on Joe's desk rang. "Hi, it's Sara."

"Wait a minute, I'll put you on speaker; hey, Bill, over here. OK, whadja find?"

"You were on the mark, Joe! We found traces of a glue compound that could be inhaled, either as a fine powder or as fumes if the cocaine was heated over a flame. It's pretty nasty stuff and could cause kidney failure, brain damage, pulmonary problems, and possibly even cardiac arrhythmia. The thing is, I don't know what it's doing in the cocaine."

Joe thought for a second, "Well, wouldn't a dealer use it to cut the coke? You know, make one kilo into two kilos and make some extra profit?"

"Nope, it's potent stuff, and there is not enough here mixed in to make it worthwhile to do that."

"OK, then why put it in?" asked Bill. "If a local pusher isn't cutting it to make more money, he isn't going to intentionally poison his customers. And a major supplier higher up in the food chain isn't going to risk his reputation for no reason by selling bad stuff."

"It just doesn't make sense," said Joe.

"Well, here's some good news" said Sara.

"Hit me, I need it."

"There's enough in here so that we can use it for a marker."

"A what?"

"You know, a marker, to differentiate it so you can trace a sample. Now that we know what to look for, it is easy enough to spot so that we can tell if any more coke that comes in is from this same source."

"I guess we should be happy for good news," said Joe.

Chapter 11

Cozumel, Mexico

It was 8:30 in the morning as Carl Olsen stood on the pier next to the Palancar Princess hotel with his wife, Nora, and two children, Melissa, age fifteen, and Tommy, twelve, waiting for their boat to pick them up for their morning dives. Their scheduled pick-up time was 9:00, but they loved being ready early so they could enjoy the view from the dock and watch the boats of the local dive operation, Playa Divers, being equipped for their morning diving trips. Divers were already boarding several boats, excited with anticipation of experiencing the bountiful variety of marine life that lay beneath the surface of Cozumel's pristine waters.

Each member of the Olsen family enjoyed this time in their own special way: Carl enjoyed watching the steady parade of boats filled with divers, speeding from the central and northern part of the island to the dive sites located toward the southern end of Cozumel. By noon, the parade would reverse itself as the boats returned to pick up new divers for afternoon diving. Nora loved to absorb the panoramic view, which was especially dramatic in the morning, when the brilliant sun shone on a cobalt blue sea, which met an azure sky at the horizon. The colors were made all the more vibrant by the crystal clear early morning air. She turned to face the gentle sea breeze and closed her eyes as she took a deep breath. Savoring the freshness of the sweet-smelling air, Nora felt totally alive.

The family lived in St. Louis, Missouri, and, having been raised in the land-locked, mid-western part of the United States, Nora never tired of the beauty of the Caribbean. Tommy liked to watch the hustle and bustle of the dive operation, and he especially liked hearing the clinking and clanking sound of the scuba tanks being carried from the air-fill station out to the boats. Melissa had recently discovered that, unlike earlier vacations, she was now a subject of attention from the younger members of the dive staff and she was spending her time simply enjoying the attention and admiring glances.

While Carl watched the steady stream of dive boats passing by, one of the boats suddenly peeled off and headed straight for the pier. They watched the dive boat knife through the water and, as it came closer, they recognized the familiar form of Terry Hunter standing next to Pepe, the mate on the boat. Today, her long hair was tied back in a bun for diving. Watching her as the boat pulled alongside the dock, Carl wondered why she was still not married, or otherwise attached, but he knew very little of Terry's background, other than she was twenty-nine, a native Californian who had transplanted herself into Mexico several years earlier and decided to stay as the roots took. He also knew that she was a first-rate scuba instructor, who referred to her customers as "students" because she enjoyed teaching, not only scuba skills but also about undersea marine life. The depth and breadth of her knowledge rivaled that of many marine biologists.

The Olsen family had never done very much long-distance traveling until a couple of years ago, just after their first trip to Cozumel, when they discovered diving. They had taken a sample dive lesson that year from Terry, who was one of the Playa Divers instructors at that time. Everyone loved the experience so much that they made a family decision to become certified divers so they could explore and enjoy the undersea world together.

Consequently, they returned the following year and took the full open water certification course from Terry, who had become a family friend.

Prior to that, most of their vacations involved visiting family in other parts of Missouri, camping in the lakes and parks, and the obligatory trip that all families with young children must eventually make – the pilgrimage to Walt Disney World in Orlando, Florida. There just never seemed to be enough money in the budget for exotic vacations. No one complained, though. Nora made sure that everyone had a good time and the important thing was to be together.

She could tell that Carl had been chafing, however, that he wanted something more. *Oh well, a little deprivation was good if it created more ambition,* she reasoned, *it made one strive and work harder,* her mid-western, American heartland work ethic told her. The incentive must have worked, because after their first trip to Cozumel, there was more money to go on more vacations. Nora and Carl discussed their improved financial position one evening over coffee after the children had gone to bed. Carl explained that his business had expanded and become more profitable due to the addition of some major new accounts that he had worked hard to secure.

Now that they had the means, she wished that they could travel to other exotic locales, but for some reason Carl wanted to keep returning to Cozumel. *Oh well, if you have to be somewhere this is a pretty nice place to be,* she mused. Without Nora realizing it, the financially lean times had transformed her into the master, or mistress, of rationalization and compromise. On this year's vacation, however, they would not be diving with Playa Divers. Terry had left Playa Divers last year to start her own business, so this year, over Carl's objections, they were diving with a different operation: *DiveWithTerry.*

"Hi, Terry," yelled Melissa and Tommy, as Pepe threw a line to fasten Terry's boat, the *Dorado,* to the dock.
"Hey, gang, great to see you! Let's go diving!" responded Terry, in her usual upbeat fashion.

"Wow, cool boat, Terry," Tommy gushed, being the first one to jump aboard. "How much did it cost? Hey dad, can we get one?" Nora rolled her eyes and Carl diplomatically said, "A little expensive for us, son, especially with no place to use it back home." Terry just laughed.

"Too much money for me, too, Tommy," she said. "Our captain, Manuel, actually owns the boat, I just rent it from him for my dive trips." Tommy eyeballed Manuel, trying to figure out how old he was. In fact, he was 47 years old, but his sun-tanned, wind-blown skin made him look at least 10 years older. He was one of the best dive boat captains in Cozumel, very experienced in finding dive sites, reading currents and, most importantly, following the bubbles of the divers so the boat would be near when they surfaced. This is a very important skill, especially in Cozumel, where drift-diving with the currents is the norm. An inexperienced captain who could not read the currents or track the divers could end up a mile or more from where the divers might surface.

Terry made a quick check to be sure everyone had all their equipment with them before departing for the reef. Everyone had their mask, snorkel, fins and booties, and Pepe hooked up the rest of their equipment, air regulator, air and depth gauges, and buoyancy compensating device, onto their scuba tanks.

"Do you guys have any preference for where we dive today?" asked Terry. No one did, so Terry selected Paso del Cedral Reef. "Since it's your first dive since last year, I'm making this a relatively easy, single-tank dive, not too deep, between 40 and 60 feet, with a good variety of fish and coral to see, possibly with an occasional hawksbill turtle or nurse shark thrown in as a bonus. You'll be diving all week, so no need to rush things the first day. Tomorrow we can do a two-tank dive. The current can be moderately strong here but it looks mild today." The Olsens nodded their assent to Terry's plan.

The *Dorado* moved easily through the channel and, after only 10 minutes, they arrived at Paso del Cedral Reef. "OK, gang, we're here," said Terry, "Let's go over the dive plan. I want to make sure that everyone understands what we will do on this dive, highlight any potential dangerous situations particular to the area and reinforce our safety procedures."

Terry began the dive plan: "We'll descend together to the bottom at about 50 feet and follow the natural line of the reef going no deeper than 60 feet. You can stop along the way to look at something interesting, but make sure you stay with your buddy! I checked your tanks before we left this morning and you all have a full load of 3000psi, but check it again when you turn on your air valve. Look at your air gauge every couple of minutes; when the first person gets down to 700 pounds of air, let me know and we will begin to slowly ascend to our safety stop at fifteen feet, where we will stay for three to five minutes before proceeding to the surface. Look up before you surface to ensure there are no boats moving above you. At the surface, press the inflator button to inflate your BC so you can float easily while the boat comes to pick you up. Everyone understand? Any questions? OK, everyone get your equipment on."

Pepe helped Carl and Nora as Terry assisted Melissa and Tommy while Manuel kept the *Dorado* in position over the reef. When everyone was ready, Terry performed a last-minute safety check on each diver: "BCs hooked up properly to regulators and tanks? Straps and buckles fastened? Weights adjusted and comfortable? Air turned on? BCs inflated? OK, you're ready to go! We'll be doing a backward roll into the water, so two divers sit on each side of the boat in order to keep the boat balanced, with your backs to the water. When Pepe counts 3-2-1-Go, we all roll backwards into the water together."

When everyone was positioned properly, Pepe counted, "3-2-1-Go!" Everyone rolled into the water and quickly bobbed to the surface as planned, due to the positive buoyancy of their inflated BCs. Terry gathered the group together and asked, "Is everyone OK?" Everybody indicated they were ready to descend. "OK, let's go down." All the divers held the end of the inflation /deflation hose of their BCs above their heads and pressed the deflation button. As the air was released from their BCs they became negatively buoyant and slowly began to descend, as if they were on an elevator going down into another world. Each diver equalized his or her ears every few feet and, after a few minutes, everyone had reached to the planned depth and began to explore the reef together.

For this dive, Carl and Nora had decided to buddy-up with each of the kids. Carl took Tommy and Nora took Melissa: guys and gals. Terry was happy with the arrangement. Although she maintained her vigilance over her charges, like a mother hen over her chicks, the fact that the more experienced parents were paired with each child enabled Terry to relax a bit and enjoy the dive.

Terry heard the sound of someone signaling by banging something metallic against their scuba tank. She turned around and saw Tommy excitedly pointing past her right shoulder. She looked where he was pointing and saw an eagle ray with a four-foot "wing span" cruising by, then banking left like an airplane, and crossing in front of her and Tommy. They gave chase and followed the beautifully spotted animal for a minute, but were quickly outdistanced, even though it appeared that the ray was swimming in a graceful, relaxed manner. Tommy's dad, his dive buddy, was following close by and quickly caught up. Terry indicated that the group should reassemble and check their air gauges.

They assembled in a patch of sand at a depth of 40 feet, surrounded by coral heads, and each diver indicated to Terry using sign language how much air each had left. They had been underwater for about 40 minutes and Carl Olsen was the lowest at 900psi, so Terry indicated that they should continue their dive, but at continually shallower depths.

After about ten minutes, the group reached 15 feet and Terry motioned for them to hold at this depth for their safety-stop of about five minutes. As they hovered, weightless in the water, it was a good time to relax, just hang out and watch the sea life. Sometimes the most interesting things were seen during a safety-stop. Terry thought back to a dive last year, when a large manta ray, rarely seen in this area, cruised by, only 20 feet under her dive group during their safety stop.

After about five minutes, Terry gave the Olsen family a thumbs-up sign, indicating that they could surface. When they reached the surface, Terry reminded the group to inflate their BCs so it would be easier to float in the few minutes it took the boat to reach them. In addition, they would be more visible floating higher in the water, minimizing the possibility that a passing boat might hit someone. Manuel skillfully guided the boat to the divers and Pepe assisted them up the ladder and into the boat. Terry asked, "Well, how was the dive?"

"Totally awesome!" exclaimed Tommy. "Did you guys see the eagle ray?"

"No, but did you see the nurse shark swimming along the bottom?" asked Melissa, not to be outdone by her little brother. Terry smiled at the give-and-take of sibling rivalry and, for a brief moment, wondered what her children might have been like if she and Mark had been given the opportunity to have had a family.

After a 20-minute ride, the Olsen family was dropped off at their hotel pier and Terry instructed them to leave their dive gear on board so she and Pepe could rinse off the salt water and set it up in preparation for the next day's diving – another personal service of *DiveWithTerry*. "So long, guys. See you tomorrow, same time, same place," said Terry. "OK, Pepe, shove off and let's get home."

Homeport for the Dorado was the marina at Puerto De Albrigo, another 30-minute boat ride north. Once there, Terry and Pepe would unload the empty tanks and prepare the dive gear for rinsing and set-up. She had a gray pick-up truck that was perfect for transporting dive gear. They loaded up the truck and Terry dropped Pepe off on her way home. "See you tomorrow, Pepe. Good job today." Pepe smiled at Terry's praise and waved back. As he turned to go into his apartment, he thought, *I am so lucky; how many people can say that they love their boss?*

Back in their hotel room, Nora talked about the day's diving with Carl. "Now aren't you glad that the kids and I insisted in booking our diving with Terry this year instead of with Playa Divers, dear? The kids love her and she always looks after all of us. I just feel much safer than being on a larger boat with ten other divers."

"Yeah, I guess so," Carl responded grudgingly. He couldn't argue with her logic, but he missed hanging around with his newfound pals at Playa Divers.

"I just don't know what you see in those guys, and that Oscar character gives me the creeps!"

"They're not so bad," Carl deflected. "I'm going down to see what the kids are doing in the pool and get a drink; see ya later," he said as he left. He wasn't in a mood for this discussion today.

"I'll join you in a..." was all Nora could say before the door closed. *Oh well, I guess Carl needs some space today*, she rationalized.

She looked where he was pointing and saw an eagle ray with a four-foot "wing span" cruising by, then banking left like an airplane, and crossing in front of her and Tommy.

Photo by Paul J. Mila

Chapter 12

Terry was up early to prepare for today's diving. First, she checked that day's work schedule. The only job she had booked was diving with the Olsen family. Usually, she had dive parties booked for both the morning and afternoon dives, but for some reason this was a light week. That's how it went when you had your own business – slow times and busy times. Terry didn't mind the slow times as long as they were not too frequent. They allowed her to catch up on personal things. Then she checked her e-mail, and paper mail, packed snacks for the surface interval between the first and second dives, and then got in her truck for the drive to the marina, where she would meet Pepe and Manuel.

At the marina, Terry and Pepe picked up the fresh air tanks she had ordered the night before from the fill station, packed the dive gear onto the boat and set off for the Palancar Princess dock with captain Manuel at the helm. He expertly guided the *Dorado* out of the slip and through the narrow passage that separated the boat slips from the main channel and headed south. As usual, the Olsen family was early, waiting on the pier. As they boarded, Carl Olsen asked Terry, "Well, what's on the schedule for today?"

"We're doing a two-tank dive today; a deep dive first, then a leisurely surface interval, and then a shallower dive. For our first dive, the deep one, I thought you might like to dive on a wreck," said Terry.

"Awesome!" exclaimed Tommy. Terry sometimes wondered if his vocabulary included any other words. Carl and Nora Olsen looked at each other apprehensively.

"I really don't think it's a good idea to dive that wreck, Terry," Carl said, in a surprisingly strident tone.

"Aw, come on, Dad. It'll be cool," said Tommy.

"I'd like to see it, too," chimed in Melissa. Carl shot Nora a look, asking for support with his eyes, but she also wanted to see the wreck and her mind was racing to come up with a compromise solution or a rationalization for some course of action.

"It's very safe," said Terry. "It's the only dive site on the island with a mooring buoy, so we can descend and ascend in a very controlled fashion on a line that is fastened to the wreck. The wreck's resting upright in about 80 feet of water but if you don't feel comfortable going that deep we can just swim along the top of the wreck at about 60 feet. Before it was sunk, the government cut several large holes through the sides so divers can enter and exit the wreck safely. You can always see daylight, unless you go down a dark passageway, which I *don't* allow my divers to do."

"Well, if you think it's safe for us, that's OK by me, and anyway, I guess I'm outvoted," said Carl as his wife nodded her agreement.

"What kind of ship is it? What's the name?" asked Tommy.

"It's an old mine sweeper that was also used for coastal patrol work. The Mexican government intentionally sank it recently to provide a habitat for the fish and hopefully to grow coral and become part of the reef system. So far, there's only a little coral on the wreck but there are lots of hydroids growing on it and plenty of fish to see," Terry explained.

"Awesome!"

"It's called the *Felipe Xicotencatl*." Terry was careful to pronounce the last name properly, phonetically sounding like, *Sheeko-ten-kattel*, but

Carl and Nora noticed Manuel and Pepe laughing. "What's the joke all about?" asked Nora.

"Well, the locals kind of butcher the name," explained Terry, "So, *Xicotencatl* sounds like, *'Shit-N-Tinkle'*." That got giggles from Melissa and Tommy and an embarrassed smile from Nora. "For our second, shallower dive, I thought we would explore Chankanaab Reef, just off Chankanaab National Park. It's an easy dive."

Soon, they reached the dive site of the wreck of the *Felipe Xicotencatl*. They agreed that everyone could handle the maximum depth of 80 feet, so Terry went over the dive plan. "OK, this time we are using a descent line so when we are ready to descend, swim over to the line. I'll go first, so follow me. Just hold the line as you go down slowly, equalizing your ears as you go. The water is very clear today so you will see the wreck as soon as you are under water. When you get within a few feet of the bow, let go of the line and swim to the bottom with me. We'll swim along the bottom at 80 feet, toward the stern where you will be able to see the ship's propeller. Look for a large grouper that usually hangs out there."

"Awesome!"

"Then we swim up along to the left side at about 60 feet and move toward the bow. At mid-ships you will see some large cut-outs in the hull. We'll go inside and through the rooms and out the other side, then up to the deck at about 50 feet. You can have some fun going into the wheelhouse to take pictures if you brought a camera, you can hold onto the bow railing, you can go up to the crow's nest, and then when the first person is down to 700 pounds of air we'll go over to the line and up to fifteen feet for our safety stop for three to five minutes. Then we surface. Any questions? OK, suit up and let's go diving!"

The group descended and the sunken ship was clearly visible as soon as they submerged. They reached the bottom and began swimming toward the stern. Right next to the ship's propeller was a huge grouper, almost four feet long, just hanging out as Terry had promised. She looked at Tommy and exchanged the diver's "OK" sign. Terry knew he would have said "Awesome" had he not been 80 feet underwater. Working their way up to the side of the ship they entered through one of the holes cut into the port side, large enough to permit easy entry and exit.

Once inside the ship, Terry noticed something odd. A few fish were swimming in disoriented fashion, some in circles, some on their side or even upside down, bouncing along the bottom of the deck as if they could not control their buoyancy or equilibrium. Odd, she thought, as she continued the dive and made a mental note to check this out at a later time. No one else seemed to notice, but Terry saw Carl looking intently at the disoriented fish, with an expression that she could not make out through his facemask. She wondered, *was it concern? Puzzlement? Fear?*

They exited through the starboard side and then explored the main deck, wheelhouse and bridge. After 50 minutes it was time to surface and the group ascended up the line to fifteen feet and hovered for five minutes. Melissa was frantically pointing to something below and they looked down, mesmerized, as an unusually large southern stingray, with a "wing span" of almost five feet, glided by, thirty feet below them.

Back on the boat, they all exchanged observations about the dive as Manuel headed for the site Terry had selected for their required surface interval, near their next dive site. The surface interval is a required period of time that divers must remain at the surface before the next dive, usually from thirty minutes to an hour, depending on time and depth of the previous dive. This ensures that their bodies have sufficient time to expel, or, "off-gas," any residual nitrogen in their bloodstream. Diving again too soon after a dive would mean that the diver would begin the next dive with excess nitrogen still in his body, increasing the possibility that too much nitrogen could accumulate in the body. The result could be decompression sickness, "the bends." The surface interval is also a relaxing time, when divers can socialize, sleep, sun bathe, check their equipment, have some refreshments, whatever. Terry always provided her divers with water or soft drinks for hydration and a light snack for nourishment.

On the way, Terry commented on the strange behavior of the fish inside the wreck, but Carl said, "Really, I didn't notice anything unusual. It was an interesting dive, though." *Strange,* Terry thought, making another mental note, *it sure looked to me like those fish got his undivided attention.*

There was no dock at the site of their second dive, so Manuel dropped the boat's anchor as soon as he was sure he was over a sand flat and not a patch of coral, which could be destroyed by the falling anchor. They still had some time to kill, so Manuel and Pepe jumped in for a quick dip to cool off while Tommy and Melissa debated over who had seen the coolest stuff on the last dive. They were near Chankanaab Reef, located just off the Chankanaab National Park area. Terry selected it because it would be a shallow dive, 40 to 50 feet, and there would be an abundance of marine life. She checked the time of their elapsed surface interval on her dive computer, and when it was safe to dive they reviewed the dive plan, jumped in and submerged.

It was their best dive so far. There were beautiful, colorful sponges of varying shapes, numerous coral formations, and everywhere they turned they saw a multitude of colorful fish. There was a wide variety of angel fish, set off from the other fish by their shape, like swimming discs: French angels, black with a distinctive gold, herring-bone pattern, multi-colored, blue and yellow queen angelfish, inquisitive grey angels that approached the divers and then followed them. They saw schools of yellow-tail snappers, jacks, parrotfish and many others.

As they swam past a huge, five-foot tall, rust-colored barrel sponge, they came upon a large, old barracuda, who eyed them warily as it hovered over a formation of brain coral, red pillar coral, and yellow tube sponges. The old fish, almost five feet long, confident in his position as the top predator of this reef, allowed them to approach to within several feet before turning to face them with a toothsome challenge. Terry knew at once that this was a display of dominance, which would be soon followed by a charge. She motioned the group to quickly, but deliberately, move on. Tommy and Melissa, both wide-eyed with excitement at being so close to such a dangerous fish, promptly obeyed.

Halfway through the dive, Terry noticed some fleeting shadows in the distance and banged on her tank to get the group's attention. A pod of dolphins was speeding past, purposefully it seemed, probably searching for their next meal. She pointed them out and the group watched briefly as they seemed to glide effortlessly through the water. When they were almost out of sight, two dolphins suddenly peeled off from the group and swam toward the divers. As they got closer, they adjusted course and buzzed by Terry, almost spinning her around. Terry couldn't believe her luck, for the benefit of the Olsen family. A close encounter with wild dolphins! They were wild dolphins, but these two were not strangers. Terry recognized them as a mature female, Notchka, and her two-year old son, Lucky, and they recognized Terry, which was why they had decided to pay her an impromptu visit while they were swimming through the area.

Two years earlier, while Terry was still working for Playa Divers, she had come upon the pair, a large, mature female dolphin and a six-month old calf. Somehow, the calf had become partially entangled in a fishing net and was having trouble swimming. He would either eventually tire and drown or grow weak from an inability to catch food and slowly starve to death. The mother was unable to free her calf, despite her best attempts to pull the net off with her teeth. Terry was able to approach him because he was simply too exhausted to swim away. At first the mother dolphin attempted to keep her body between Terry and her calf, but then must have sensed that this strange-looking creature that blew bubbles meant no harm and allowed Terry access.

Terry had been careful to unwind the net slowly, since it had started to dig into the sensitive skin of the baby dolphin. The dolphin squealed in pain as Terry worked and the mother became more agitated. Then, sensing that Terry was helping, the mother moved next to her baby's head and began directing a series of audible sounds directly at her calf. In response, the baby dolphin seemed to relax, which made Terry's job easier and, in a few more minutes, the offending net was off. The young dolphin, free for the first time in several weeks, celebrated its freedom by swimming rapidly in circles around Terry and then moved next to its mother. Before swimming off, the mother dolphin placed it beak, or rostrum, several feet from Terry's facemask and directed a stream of clicks and whistles directly to her. Terry could only assume that this was "dolphinese" for "thank you."

Terry had noticed that the female had a large notch in her tail, probably due to a too-close encounter with a shark or some other predator. She was going to name her "Notch" but decided that sounded too masculine.

"Notchka" seemed more appropriately feminine. She named the calf "Lucky" because that's what he was: lucky that Terry had happened upon him and saved his life. Since that time, whenever this pod of about twenty or thirty dolphins was in the area, Notchka and Lucky would break off from the group for a few minutes to see if Terry was in the area. Consequently, they had short reunions several times per year.

Terry and the Olsen family had fun with the dolphins for a few minutes before they departed to rejoin the main pod, and the divers ascended to 15 feet for their safety stop and then ended the dive. As they bobbed in the water while Manuel maneuvered the boat to pick them up they were ecstatic. "Whoa, dolphins! Cool!" said Melissa.

"Oh Carl, Tommy, wasn't that an unbelievable experience?" Nora gushed.

"Awesome!"

"Not many divers ever get a chance to have a wild dolphin encounter," said Terry, "You guys are certainly a lucky bunch!"

Manuel steered the *Dorado* back to the Palancar Princess pier and then proceeded to the dock at the marina in Puerto De Albrigo. Terry decided to go back to her apartment and get some rest. On her sun porch, she unwound with a bottle of cold chablis and reflected on the last dive. As much as she had enjoyed seeing Notchka and Lucky again, it was a bittersweet experience because it reminded her of the reason for her departure from Playa Divers and of the incident that had soon followed, which had almost ruined her life two years ago.

.... they came upon a large, old barracuda, who eyed them warily as it hovered over an interesting formation of brain coral, red pillar coral and yellow tube sponges.

Photo by Paul J. Mila
© All Rights Reserved

Chapter 13

Cozumel,

Two Years Earlier

Terry's success after leaving Playa Divers had been more rapid than she had anticipated, and after only several months she had too much business to handle alone. She realized that she would have to hire a mate to assist her in loading and unloading scuba tanks, rinsing and setting up equipment, and other work that needed to be done.

One day as she was getting ready to advertise for an assistant, Ramon Diaz, one of the assistants at Playa Divers, unexpectedly showed up at the dock when the *Dorado* was coming in from a day of diving. "Hola, senorita Terry," he called out to her.

"Hola, Ramon, nice to see you." They had gotten along well at Playa Divers and Terry liked him. "What's up, Ramon, why aren't you at work?"

"I had a fight with Oscar over my pay and he fired me. Any chance that you could use me?" For Terry, the timing could not have been better. Ramon was a known quantity, a hard worker, and customers liked him. He would be a good addition to *DiveWithTerry.*

"OK, consider yourself hired as of right now. Help me with this equipment. I'm ready to collapse."

The arrangement worked out very well. Terry, Manuel, and Ramon were a good team and business was booming as more former Playa Divers customers learned that *DiveWithTerry* was up and running.

One morning, the customers on the *Dorado* included a diver who Terry couldn't believe was really certified. Mr. Bob Dixon, from Houston, Texas, was so overweight that he required 32 pounds of lead to get him underwater, so out of shape that he was out of breath after a few minutes of treading water, and generally uncoordinated. Still, he had his "C-card," the certification card signifying that one is a trained diver. Being cautious, Terry decided to give him a quick checkout of basic skills. He passed, but just barely. Terry decided she would keep an extra sharp eye on him; she would be his dive buddy.

As Terry and three other divers began to descend, Dixon lagged behind, having difficulty clearing his ears and establishing correct buoyancy. Then Terry could see he was having trouble breathing and was in the early stages of a panic attack. Panic is a diver's deadliest enemy, impairing judgment and creating physical difficulties if it gets out of control. The other two divers were experienced, advanced divers and having no trouble, so Terry signaled them to stay put on the bottom until she returned. She escorted Dixon slowly to the surface, inflated his BC for him to help him float and asked him if he was OK. He said that he was, so Terry told Ramon to assist him in getting on the boat, and she returned to the other divers.

Ramon could see that the diver was too heavy and unfit to climb the ladder wearing his equipment, so he explained that he would have to take it off in the water and then climb aboard. By this time, Dixon was relaxed enough to follow Ramon's directions. "First, senor, remove your fins and hand them to me." Manuel, who was up on the bridge, turned around to see what was happening. "Now unbuckle your BC and hand it to me."

Manuel quickly stepped down from the bridge toward Ramon and the diver. Everything else happened very quickly. When Dixon unbuckled his inflated BC he began having difficulty staying afloat, and as soon as he handed it to Ramon he sunk like a rock, with 32 pounds of lead on his weight belt pulling him down. Manuel and Ramon watched helplessly through the clear water, seeing the diver looking up as he was plunging toward the bottom 80 feet away, frantically clawing at the surface, but to no avail. All he had to do to save himself was to ditch his weights by simply pulling the release buckle on his weight belt with one hand, as divers are trained to do in such situations, but the sudden panic blocked from his mind what little training he had. There was no other dive equipment on the boat, so diving in to save him was out of the question. Manuel radioed for assistance, even as he tracked the bubbles of the other divers, who would not surface for another thirty minutes. News of a missing diver travels rapidly in any diving community. Terry and the other two divers surfaced to find a Mexican Coast Guard cutter alongside the *Dorado* and a helicopter hovering overhead.

"What the hell's going on, Ramon?" Terry asked, seeing an officer from the cutter questioning a very shaken Manuel, and not immediately realizing that one passenger was missing from her boat. Ramon said, "Senor Dixon sank with his weight belt on, I fear he has drowned." Terry and the other divers immediately replaced the spent tanks with fresh ones that were to be used for the second dive. They had not taken a required surface interval yet, so Terry said, "Don't go lower than 20 feet. If we spot him on the bottom, I'll go down and get him!" She was willing to risk her life, but not the lives of the other divers. Because the current was moderately strong, the boat had drifted hundreds of yards since the accident, so Manuel could not be sure exactly where the unfortunate diver had gone down.

They searched the area by swimming in a "box" pattern, a common search-and-rescue technique, where divers swim a pre-determined length and then make 90-degree turns until the search area has been covered in the square shape of a box, but to no avail. When they surfaced, an officer on the cutter wanted to speak with Terry, so she instructed Manuel to take the *Dorado* and the rest of the dive party back to shore while she accompanied the authorities back on the cutter.

Mr. Dixon was presumed drowned and missing – for now. They all knew that in the warm Caribbean water a dead body would quickly start to decompose and the resulting internal gases in the body would bring it, even though weighted down, bloated to the surface. Two days later, Mr. Dixon, much larger than when he was last seen alive, washed up onto a nearby beach, named San Francisco, only a few miles from where he had drowned.

Clearly, there would be an investigation. A location such as Cozumel, which depends on diving to support the local economy, cannot afford to get a bad reputation for safety, especially in a sport were the consequences of an accident can be fatal. A poorly managed dive operation cannot be tolerated and Terry knew that the outcome of the investigation would determine her future on Cozumel. At the hearing, Terry was questioned and explained her version of what had transpired. When Ramon was called to testify, Terry leaned forward and listened intently.

"Please state your name and residence."

"Ramon Diaz. I live in the town of San Miguel."

"You were the mate on board the Dorado on the day that senor Dixon died?"

"Yes."

"Please tell the court what happened."

"I was on the boat, and all of a sudden senorita Terry and senor Dixon came to the surface. I knew something was wrong because it was too soon. As soon as they surfaced I could see that senor Dixon was in some kind of trouble. He was gasping for air and asked senorita Terry to help him, but she said she had to get back to the other divers." Terry was stunned and shocked. She jumped up and exclaimed,

"He's lying!"

"Please sit down, Miss Hunter! Continue, please, senor Diaz."

"I asked him to take off his weight belt first, but instead he unbuckled his BC. He started to sink and I tried to reach for him but all I could grab was the BC, which slipped off and then he went down."

"Thank you for your testimony. You have been most helpful."

84

Terry sat frozen in shock, anger and disbelief. She was also hurt. *How could he turn on me? Why would he lie?* She had helped him, given him a job after Oscar had fired him. *Oscar?* Had Oscar really fired him? Or had he sent Ramon on a mission? Terry's head began spinning as she realized what was happening. Oscar had vowed to ruin her, to crush her, to destroy her. Who would the authorities believe? Ramon Diaz, a native of Cozumel, who, as far as they knew, had no motive to give false testimony? He was simply a deck hand. It was Terry Hunter's responsibility for running a safe dive operation. If anyone had a reason to cover up a mistake, it was she, and she was an outsider. Terry could see all her work and dreams crumbling, as she would be driven out of Cozumel in scandal and disgrace, if not imprisoned first. She held her head in her hands as Manuel Perez, captain of the *Dorado*, took the stand. She had tried to reach Manuel, but had not seen or heard from him since the accident, two days earlier. She listened apprehensively.

"Please state your name and residence for the court."
"Manuel Lopez. I live in San Miguel, Cozumel."
"You were the captain on the day that senor Dixon died?"
"Yes."
"Please tell the court what happened that day."
"Two divers surfaced early, so I wondered why. I saw it was senorita Terry and senor Dixon. She asked him if he was OK and he said yes. Senorita Terry told Ramon to help him into the boat and she returned to the other divers." Terry looked up and watched Manuel, through tears.
"What happened next?"
"Senor Dixon handed Ramon his fins, and then his BC. As soon as he handed his BC to Ramon, he sunk below the waves."
"He took his equipment off in that order?" This was the reverse order for removing equipment in the water. First the weights come off, then the BC, and the fins are removed last, in the event the diver gets separated from the boat and must swim.
"Yes, because Ramon Diaz told him to do it that way!"
The courtroom exploded into chaos. Terry jumped up as Ramon shouted at Manuel, "Liar! You could not possibly know what I told him to do. You don't understand English!" The judge pounded his gavel.
"Silence! Order!"

The judge looked at Manuel, whom he had known for many years. "Manuel, can you understand English?"

In heavily accented, but very understandable, English, Manuel proudly said, "Yes I can, and, as you can hear for yourself, I can also speak English." The special favor that Manuel had asked from Terry that night in his apartment a year ago was for her to teach him English in exchange for his agreement to rent her his boat. He wanted to travel to the United States someday when he had saved enough money, and when he went he wanted be able to speak English. Terry had been teaching him once or twice a week over the past year and, luckily for her, he had been a very attentive student. For reasons know only to Manuel, however, he had never used his English in public, so no one ever knew he could understand or speak the language.

The judge looked sternly at Ramon Diaz, who had made himself as small as he could in his chair. "Senor Diaz, please return to the witness stand." Terry's eyes blazed at him over his treachery. On his second visit to the witness stand, Ramon broke down under strong questioning and testified that Oscar had put him up to working for Terry, in order to perform some act of sabotage in the hope of ruining her business.

In the end, Ramon was sentenced to a long prison term, but nothing could be proven against Oscar. Terry felt somewhat sorry for Ramon. He was just a kid, a pawn of Oscar, who had now ruined Ramon's life and almost ruined Terry's life. But she had survived and built a thriving business.

Chapter 14

Cozumel

Present Day

Sipping her wine on the sun porch of her apartment after the day's diving with the Olsen family had relaxed Terry, even as she thought about Ramon's testimony during his second visit to the witness stand, almost two years ago, which had revealed how far Oscar would go to destroy her.

Today had been a busy day, a good day of diving. Seeing Notchka and Lucky had been fun, but something about the dive today was still rattling around in her mind, bothering her. *What was it?* Then she remembered: the fish that she had seen in the wreck of the *Felipe Xicotencatl.* Terry wondered, *Why where they swimming so strangely?* She would have to go back and check it out when she had a chance. For now, she was tired, and sleep came easily after a physically exhausting day.

PART II

Resolution

Chapter 15

Merrick, Long Island

Joe Manetta went to answer the doorbell. "Detective Manetta? Sorry to disturb you, sir; may we come in?"

"Sure, come on in. What's up, fellas?"

"Sir, I'm sorry, but we have some very bad news for you."

Suddenly Joe heard a phone ringing and as he reached across the bed to answer it, he realized he had been having the nightmare again. "Hello," Joe mumbled groggily into the mouthpiece.

"Hey, Joe, Bill here. Sorry to wake you at this hour, buddy." Joe looked over at the alarm clock, 3am.

"It's OK, Bill. What's up?" Actually, Joe wanted to thank Bill for waking him up before he got to the worst part of the nightmare, the part where he was at the morgue identifying the broken remains of his family.

"Hey, we got a break! A big tractor-trailer, an 18-wheeler, carrying fruit and other produce, jack-knifed coming off the Verrazano Bridge in Brooklyn. He sideswiped a small sports car and it got caught under the truck. The driver of the car didn't make it."

"What a damn shame," said Joe. Hearing about fatal traffic accidents always unsettled him, as he thought about the effect on whomever would be soon receiving the bad news. "What else, Bill?"

"So, what else is that one of the uniforms at the scene spotted some white powder leaking out from one of the spare tires on the underside of the trailer where the sports car was wedged. He sent it to the lab and, luckily for us, your friend Sara Flynn was working late and tested for the glue, in addition to running the standard tests."

"And?"

"And bingo! Not only was it cocaine, but it also tested positive for the glue, so now we know how our stuff is getting up here."

"Where did the load originate?"

"The driver said he came up from Miami on 95."

"Miami! Now that's the first thing that has made sense in this case so far." Miami is one of the major drug importation centers in the Unites States; a drug hub, actually, since the distribution networks from locations like Miami fanned out across the country like the spokes of a wheel. "You said we had the driver?"

"Yeah, and his co-pilot, too."

"Are we talking to them?"

"Yeah, they're being interrogated downtown." That sounded better than just being interviewed, thought Joe.

"Let's get down there a-sap. I'll be there in about 40 minutes." As Joe was getting dressed, he looked at another family photo on the bedroom wall. This was a family beach photo, taken on a summer Saturday afternoon at Jones Beach, one of Long Island's world-class beaches. Joe had loved riding the waves and body-surfing with the kids. They were all water bugs. He took a deep breath, thinking about how much he missed those days with his family. As soon as Joe got on the highway he put the department's Crown Vic into high gear and turned on the flashers and siren; he made it in thirty-five minutes.

Joe saw Bill already standing between the windows of the two interrogation rooms, watching the truck driver and his assistant being questioned separately. "Are they talking yet?" Joe asked.

"No, but they will soon. We have a lot of leverage in this situation. The driver is also the owner-operator, so the rig is his life. He isn't in a position to say it's just a big company rig and walk away from it. The other guy is a "guest" of our country from the Dominican Republic, with a temporary visa. Surprisingly, his paperwork is in order but he knows he doesn't have a snowball's chance in hell of staying here if he's mixed up in this and doesn't cooperate."

Joe and Bill compared notes after several hours with the suspects, playing all the classic head-games with them: one was the classic "good cop/bad cop"; another game was to create dissension: *Your partner implicated you, so why not talk instead of going down alone?* And then, Joe's favorite, the old intimidation game: leaning over with direct eye contact from a few inches away, *Listen, we already have enough evidence to put you away for a long time, so make it easy on yourself and tell us what you know.*

"OK," Joe said, "let's put it together and see what he have." Bill reviewed his notes.

"Well, my guy says that his instructions were to park the fully loaded truck at a certain rest stop on 95 North, just outside of Miami, and walk away for a couple of hours. Evidently that's when someone loaded the cocaine onto the truck. Then he'd come back to the truck and drive up to New York. After delivering the legitimate cargo to the Hunt's Point Market in the Bronx, he'd park the truck on a certain block, the location of which would change on each trip, and then walk away for a couple of hours so the pick-up could be made. Then he would come back to the truck and drive back down to Miami, to pick up another cargo of legitimate produce along with more coke."

"Yeah, my guy said pretty much the same thing. Pretty smart; so if they got pinched they never saw anything, so they couldn't tell anyone anything."

"True, but pretty dumb to use a guy who had too much to lose if he got caught. He may not know anything, but we can force him to cooperate in a stakeout, otherwise he loses his investment in his rig. They should have used a driver who just worked for a trucking company."

The two detectives conferred with their boss, Captain Barry Willis. After looking at everything they had put together, Captain Willis said, "Good job, boys. You know, if I were a betting man, I'd bet that you two will be taking a trip to Miami soon to visit our brother officers in the Miami P.D. I hear they're doing some work with the Federal Narcotics Task Force. Like, tomorrow morning. Anybody wanna bet?"

Joe and Bill slept for most of the early morning, two-and-a-half-hour flight to Miami. They were tired and the pretzel "breakfast" was not really worth waking up for.

Upon landing at Miami International Airport they checked into their hotel and Joe called their contact at the Miami Police Department. He was told that they had been assigned to a joint task force with the Miami P.D. and agents from the Federal Drug Enforcement Administration. He turned to Bill and whispered, "Hey, partner, we hit the big time. We're going to a meeting this afternoon and we get to play with the Feds."

At the meeting they were told that this smuggling investigation had been ongoing for over a year. It was revealed to the entire group that the biggest development in the case had been the lead uncovered by Joe and Bill about the strange glue mixed in with the cocaine. It could provide an accurate way to trace the route of the drugs. All they had to do was test any samples that turned up, to determine if they were following the correct trail.

Joe and Bill were appreciative that the Miami P.D. and the Feds had acknowledged the contribution made by the NYPD boys. From experience, both Joe and Bill knew that people often fought to get credit for a positive development in a situation, like sharks at a feeding frenzy. Joe tried to remember an old saying – what was it? Oh, yeah, *"Success has many fathers, while failure is an orphan."*

The task force members went over the details of a planned stakeout. The driver had cooperated in the hope of getting his rig back and his partner agreed in the hope of a deal to be able to stay in the United States. They had been instructed by the police to deliver the cargo in the Bronx as planned, but under police surveillance. The drugs were picked up, but no arrests were made, since the police did not want to tip off the drug ring. The two men were now driving down to Miami, but with an undercover police escort, just to make sure they did not make any unplanned detours.

The sting was set for the next night. The driver would park between other trucks as instructed by his boss, in order to obstruct the view of anyone watching, especially a police surveillance team. After leaving his truck at the designated location, the driver and his sidekick would leave as they always did, but this time the truck would not really be left alone. Task force members would be stationed at the entrance and exit of the rest stop. Furthermore, the trucks parked on either side of his truck were driven by police officers. A few minutes after he pulled in, the police pulled their trucks out, providing the stakeout team with a better view of the scene. *No way I could have known that would happen,* the driver could plausibly tell his boss later.

Soon, a tow-truck pulled up near the target truck and the driver rolled out a spare tire, which he simply switched for the truck's real spare. *Pretty neat,* thought Joe, *You couldn't make it look any more natural than that. Who would give a second look at something so mundane as a trucker arranging for a tire to be changed?* As soon as the switch was made, the task force moved in, arresting the surprised tow-truck driver without incident. Then they went back to their positions and, for appearance's sake, re-arrested the truck driver and his pal when they returned to the truck to make it look like they had also been busted. Police just hate to see good informers silenced by vengeful colleagues with a bullet to the back of the head.

The drugs recovered at the stakeout tested positive for the glue marker, confirming that they had uncovered one more link in the chain. How close were they to the end? The tow truck driver soon implicated his boss and, they thought, so it would go, on and on. As it turned out, however, this was the break for which the task force had been waiting.

The tow truck operator had lots of trucks in the "spare tire business" and he was a major supplier, distributing drugs to the spokes in the wheel that fanned out from Miami. He was moving hundreds, maybe thousands, of kilos per week. That meant that he would need a major supplier who could provide him with a steady flow of drugs. It looked like the team had jumped a few links in the chain and was already closing in on the source. Finally, under intense questioning and the threat of a long prison term, the tow truck owner informed the task force that he picked up his supply of cocaine in the basement of a warehouse in Miami used by several cruise lines to drop off and store supplies used for their Caribbean routes.

The task force decided against staging a high-profile raid, in the hope of breaking open an entire international drug-smuggling ring instead of just interrupting the domestic part of the operation. The following day, several task force members disguised as health department inspectors visited the warehouse under the pretense of looking for spoiling food that was causing intestinal infections among cruise ship passengers.

The "inspectors" gathered up promising samples of what looked like cocaine along with samples of totally irrelevant products. The drug samples were sent to the Miami police lab and the results confirmed that, not only was it cocaine, but it was laced with the glue marker. The task force had finally made significant progress. They had determined that the lethal drugs showing up in the streets and neighborhoods of New York were entering the country from cruise ships in Miami and then shipped north in the spare tires of long-haul tractor-trailer rigs.

Chapter 16

Cozumel

Today was the last day that the Olsen family would be diving on this year's vacation. Their flight back to St. Louis was scheduled for tomorrow afternoon. That meant that they could safely dive until late this morning, which would leave them a little over 24 hours between their last dive and their flight. That was an adequate safety margin for avoiding decompression problems if any excess nitrogen gas in the blood was released into the body due to the low atmospheric pressure of a high altitude flight.

"Hi, guys," said Terry as the *Dorado* pulled up to the Palancar Princess pier. She noticed Carl Olsen talking to Oscar at the equipment rental shack located at the opposite end of the pier. As the divers boarded, Terry could see Oscar glaring at her and she wondered if it had anything to do with his conversation with Carl. *His butt is probably burning over losing his customers to me,* Terry thought. She ignored him and resisted the temptation to look back as the *Dorado* left the pier and headed out to the reefs. "Hi, Terry. What's on the agenda for today?" asked Carl.

"Well, you're all pretty experienced now, so I thought for your last dive you would like to try some wall diving." Terry looked quickly at Tommy. Before he could open his mouth she said, "Yes, Tommy, it will be pretty awesome." They all laughed at Tommy's wide grin. "We'll dive on a part of Columbia Reef, called Columbia Deep. We'll descend to 80 feet and you'll see huge coral pillars, some 60 feet high, resembling cathedral-like columns. Follow me into the swim-throughs, which are a little like caves, but open at both ends. As we go through, look for all kinds of fish hiding under ledges and between the coral formations. On the seaward side of the coral is the wall, a vertical drop-off. Look at the sponges and corals but be careful not to go any deeper. It's easy to go deeper without realizing it because, as you're swimming along the wall, the bottom is too deep to see, so keep checking your gauges. Stay close together because the current will be moving us along. Don't fight it, just go along with it and enjoy the free ride of a drift dive. Any questions? OK, let's go diving!"

The dive was just as Terry described it. She led them around the majestic coral pillar formations and into the swim-throughs. The group seemed to fly through the water on the current, and Carl, who brought up the rear, thought they looked like the Darling family flying to Never-Never Land behind Peter Pan.

The Olsens were quiet during the boat ride back to their hotel, especially Carl, who seemed more preoccupied than usual for some reason. They were thrilled that their week of diving had gone so well, but they knew that their vacation was drawing to a close and they would probably not see Terry until next year. As the Dorado docked at the Palancar Princess pier, Melissa and Tommy hugged Terry like a big sister, while Carl and Nora thanked her for a great week of diving. As the *Dorado* pulled away, they waved goodbye to Manuel, Pepe and Terry, who yelled back, "See you next year!"

"Awesome!" shouted Tommy, as Terry laughed.

Terry asked Manuel to drive the boat slowly so she could get some additional surface time to decompress further. She wanted to make a quick dive on the wreck as long as she was in the vicinity and check on those fish. Normally, she would not make a third consecutive dive so soon after the first two, but she was taking the rest of the day off and would not be doing anymore diving this day. They tied up to the buoy moored to the wreck and, after a few more minutes of rest and relaxation, Terry descended alone, something else she did not normally do. She usually followed the diving maxim of always diving with a buddy, never alone, because you just never knew what might happen.

She descended along the mooring line and entered the wreck through the cut-out section in the side of the ship, just below the main deck. There she saw the same thing as before, a few disoriented fish. The fish population of Cozumel was normally very healthy, since the current always kept an adequate supply of nutrients and clean water flowing through the channel and across the reefs. Terry exited through the other side of the ship and then saw something else that distressed her: several dead fish floating along the bottom near the stern. She swam down and grabbed a couple, placing them into a small mesh bag that she had brought with her. They were both parrotfish, whose normally bright, beautiful colors were muted in death. They were algae eaters, obtaining the algae that they loved to eat by grazing on the coral in which the algae lived, grinding the coral with their strong beaks. In the process, new sand was created when they excreted the digested coral.

Terry swam back to the mooring line and ascended to fifteen feet for her safety stop and was glad that she had the mooring line to hold onto. The current was swift today and, as she held onto the line, she resembled a flag blowing in a stiff wind. At the surface, she handed the two dead fish to a surprised Pepe and climbed into the boat. "Let's get into town fast," she told Manuel. "I want to bring these fish to a friend of mine in the hospital lab to see if we can figure out what killed them."

Back at the marina, Terry packed the fish in ice and set off for the hospital in downtown San Miguel. She went to the office of Doctor Eduardo

Sanchez, who also doubled as the local veterinarian. "Hola, Eduardo. How are you today?"

"Hola, senorita Terry. What brings you to our facility? Are you not feeling well?"

"Oh, I'm fine, but my little friends are not," Terry said, unwrapping the dead fish. She explained the circumstances and Eduardo asked, "So you want me to perform an autopsy on a fish?"

"Well, I really want to know what killed them because, whatever it is, it's making other fish sick. If it's an infectious disease the authorities should be notified immediately." Doctor Sanchez understood the potential gravity of the situation. Some fast-spreading disease processes could wipe out the fish on the reefs, which might take years to recover. The local economy would be ruined before nature fixed the problem.

"OK, I'll examine them tonight when it is quiet here and call you as soon as I know something."

"Thanks. You're a dear," Terry said, giving him a quick hug and kissing him on the cheek as she left to go home.

Chapter 17

Task Force Headquarters

Miami Florida

The next morning, the task force met to determine their plan of attack. Two cruise ship lines used the warehouse where the drugs were found. Each line made stops throughout the Caribbean, with numerous ports of call such as Nassau, the Virgin Islands, Jamaica, Puerto Rico, Cozumel, Cancun, and the Dominican Republic, among others. The team went through the itineraries of the various cruises and two popular packages seemed to be a short cruise from Miami to Nassau, Cozumel and back to Miami and a longer cruise to the Virgin Islands, Grand Cayman, Jamaica, Cozumel and back to Miami.

Ed Butler, from the DEA, said, "Let's focus on these two cruises to start. I don't think we will learn much from being stationed on the ship. The ships are obviously picking up the stuff from one or more of these islands, so I believe the best way to proceed is to start our investigations from the most likely islands, on location, so to speak. Any comments or questions?"

Joe Manetta spoke first, "Well, except for the U.S. Virgin Islands, we may need the cooperation of foreign countries. Does that present us with any obstacles?"

"Nope; I'll get the State Department involved," said Butler, "They can smooth over the diplomatic details. Anyone else?"

"Any chance some of these governments might actually be involved in the smuggling?" another agent asked.

"That's a possibility. There's a lot of money involved, and bribery and corruption aren't exactly unknown ways of conducting business down there. It's a chance we'll just have to take. Anyone else?" No one raised any other issues. "OK, then, let's split up the assignments. For cruise number one, Nassau and Cozumel, Lopes you take Nassau, Manetta and Ryan take Cozumel, for Cruise number two, Manetta already has Cozumel covered, so Williams you take Jamaica, then,.... "

As Joe and Bill left the meeting, Bill said, "We better call the boss a-sap and let him know what the plans are. I don't think he's gonna go for it." Joe concurred.

"Chief Willis here."

"Hi chief, it's Joe; I have Bill on the other line."

"How's Florida, boys? Did you see Mickey yet?"

"That's Orlando, chief," Bill reminded him. "We're here in Miami."

"Too bad, I was hoping you might bring me back some mouse ears. OK, so what's up?" Joe filled him in on their progress. "Great, sounds like you guys are really getting closer to wrapping this mess up. What's next?" Chief Willis didn't like the next part of Joe's update. "Sorry, boys, I can't spare two of you out of the country at the same time. Tell the task force that one of you guys can go, but I need the other one back at the ranch, *pronto*."

"OK, Chief. We'll let you know who's coming back home." Joe hung up the phone and said, "Well, do you want to draw straws or flip a coin?"

"Are you kidding?" Bill laughed, "My name doesn't end in a vowel, it's 'Ryan'. Look at my baby blues and freckles. In that sun I'd look like a lobster in an hour! You're heading south, buddy."

"Hey, I don't even know where this place is. Where's a map?" Bill and Joe went over to a map on the wall of the task force's war room and looked for Cozumel. Finally Bill found it. "Here it is, off the Mexico coast, just below Cancun."

"Well, I've heard of Cancun and that's supposed to be nice, so I guess Cozumel must be OK, too."

"Hey, you goin' for a vacation or on business?" Bill said, as they both laughed.

All the next-day flights directly from Miami to Cozumel were booked, so Joe had to fly to Cancun and change to a two-engine, prop-driven "puddle-jumper" for the short fifteen-minute flight directly south to Cozumel. Joe did not fly very often, and when he did it was on large commercial jets, so when he saw the size of the plane he was a little apprehensive. As Joe boarded the aircraft and looked down the length of the short cabin, he was amazed at the cramped confines; only three seats abreast, with a single seat across the aisle from two seats. He thought it would be less claustrophobic to take a single window seat, but as he sat in his seat, he soon realized he had made a mistake.

Joe was relatively tall, at 6', and the small fuselage curved in at a sharp angle, requiring him to bend his neck toward the aisle in order to avoid bumping his head. *This better be a short flight*, Joe fumed to himself. Joe had a limited command of Spanish, having taken three years in high school plus a couple of courses in college, and he wondered what the translation for "chiropractor" was in Spanish.

Unfortunately for Joe, the scheduled fifteen-minute flight turned into thirty minutes as the small plane was forced to veer around some impressive thunderheads that had formed in the area, generated by the moist, tropical air masses created by evaporation from the warm ocean. Despite the best efforts of the pilot, the small plane was severely buffeted by the unstable air around the thunderheads and, as it bounced around the sky, Joe thought of Bill Ryan, safely back in New York, while his head was repeatedly bumped against the side of the cabin.

Disembarking at Cozumel, Joe noticed that a large U.S. Airways jet had landed moments earlier. As he watched the last of the U.S. Airways passengers entering the small terminal, he thought to himself, *I bet none of them has a bad headache like mine!* As Joe entered the terminal, he saw that the lines for Immigration and Customs were long, so he flashed his badge and entered with the crew through a specially assigned gate. At Immigration, a representative of the U.S. State Department, who had flown in from Mexico City, met Joe.

"Joe Manetta, I'm Felix Weaver, State Department. How was your flight?"

"A little bumpy," Joe said, rubbing the side of his head, "but, as they say, any landing that you walk away from is a good one."

Felix laughed and said, "Come on, I'll give you a lift and introduce you to the Mexican police officials. They are cooperating fully with us on this case." They arrived at the police station in San Miguel after a thirty-minute ride from the airport and were promptly ushered into the office of Sergeant Rafael Gonzalez.

"Welcome to Cozumel, gentlemen. I understand we will be working together on a drug-related situation that is causing your country much grief." After a round of introductions, Joe outlined the progress of the investigation for Sergeant Gonzalez and explained why the U.S. Task Force thought that Cozumel might be the source of the drugs, among other possible locations. "Well, gentlemen," Sergeant Gonzalez said, "I hope that our country is not the source of this problem, but we will, of course, help you in this investigation."

Joe listened as Felix Weaver said, "We hope so, too, Sergeant, but the Drug Enforcement Administration has become aware that, as we have increased our efforts to interdict drugs along the traditional routes through Texas and Southern California, the flow through these channels seems to have decreased. We suspect that the drug rings are using new routes, shipping the traffic eastward through Mexico and then up north to the United States."

"I see," said Sergeant Gonzalez, "Well, Detective Manetta, I will be your main point of contact. If you require any assistance, please contact me."

"Thank you. I'm sure I'll need some help along the way, so you'll be hearing from me."

"OK, thanks again," said Weaver. "Joe, let's get you checked into your hotel. I have to catch a flight back to Mexico City in two hours." Joe checked into the Hotel Lorena, a modest hotel conveniently located in town, and began planning his investigation. He was aware of a creative method used recently by heroin smugglers, which involved dissolving heroin in water and then soaking t-shirts in the solution. The shirts, which had already been stamped with designs to look like t-shirts that any tourist would buy, were then dried and then shipped into the U.S. At their final destination, the shirts were soaked in clean water and the heroin was then removed from the water, dried into bricks or left as powder and sold. Joe felt that he should try the obvious first, so he began his investigation by visiting major t-shirt importers and exporters on the island.

Chapter 18

Cozumel

Terry saw that her answering machine had four messages waiting when she came home after her morning dives with customers. The first two were from divers seeking to book time with her; the third was from an agent at one of the cruise lines trying to arrange training dives for passengers on a cruise ship that would be docking in town tomorrow morning, and the last message was from her friend, Doctor Sanchez. She played his message first.

"Hola, Terry, this is Eduardo Sanchez. I have the results of my tests on the dead parrotfish that you brought in. Please call me as soon as possible. I think you will be interested in my findings. Talk to you soon."

Terry retrieved the remainder of her messages and copied down the information so she could contact her customers. The first return call that she made was to Dr. Sanchez. "Eduardo, this is Terry, thanks for getting back to me so soon. What did you find?"

"Well, my dear, it seems your little friends were poisoned." Terry shuddered as her worst fears were confirmed. She thought of the devastating effects of various imbalances of nature, such as red tide and brown tide, which were algae blooms that killed sea life by depleting oxygen from the water, and other similar natural disasters that killed fish by producing toxins. A massive kill of local marine life would ruin the local economy for several years.

"Have you been able to identify the organisms responsible, Eduardo?"

"It seems that natural organisms are not responsible in this instance. These fish ingested drugs."

"What?!" exclaimed Terry, sitting down and running her fingers through her hair, trying to digest what she had just heard. "They were killed by drugs?"

"Well, not exactly. They had drugs in their systems, but also some kind of toxin, which I cannot identify yet. It is likely that the combination of the drugs and toxin is what killed them, although the drugs alone may have done it eventually."

"What kind of drugs?"

"I'm not totally certain, but it looks like it may have been cocaine."

"Is there anything else?"

"No, that's all I could find. Because of the drug finding I must send a report to the police, but I will send you a copy also."

"Thanks very much, Eduardo. I really appreciate your help."

"Think nothing of it, my dear Terry. I am glad to be of help. There is one more thing that I want you to consider, for your own safety. Now that illegal drugs of some kind may be involved, please be careful, OK?" This was something that Terry had never considered before.

"OK, Eduardo. I promise to be careful." She ran her hand through her hair again, trying to think about what to do next.

Later that day, Dr. Sanchez called Sergeant Rafael Gonzalez and explained the substance of the analysis that he had completed. Gonzalez' interest in the drug finding was piqued immediately, due to the recent visit from Joe Manetta and Felix Weaver, so he suggested that Sanchez bring the report over directly instead of mailing it. Sergeant Gonzalez read the report with raised eyebrows at the surprising findings. "We must investigate this as soon as possible. "Do you know where Miss Hunter found the dead fish?"

"I'm sorry, but I do not recall that she said exactly where. She may have mentioned something about diving near Chankanaab Reef, but I am not sure."

"OK," said Gonzalez, "I can contact her tomorrow and get additional details that may help our investigation. I will have to call the American detective, Manetta, and inform him of this development. Thank you for your fine work, Dr. Sanchez. If I have any more questions I will contact you."

After Sanchez left, Sergeant Gonzalez called in his staff of four senior officers to go over the report and make assignments in the investigation. Immediately after this meeting, a phone call was made from the police station to someone – someone who was responsible for enabling the caller to live far beyond the means of his police officer's salary.

"We have a serious problem that must be attended to immediately."

"Come right over. Meet me at the usual location," said the voice on the other end of the line.

Chapter 19

The next morning, as Terry's boatmate, Pepe, was walking along the road to work, he never saw the car coming up fast behind him. Pepe finally heard the car as two wheels mounted the curb but by then it was too late. As he turned, he barely saw the driver as the car ran him down and accelerated away at high speed. About a half-hour later, Terry was looking at her watch wondering why Pepe was late. *Don't be late today, of all days,* she thought, *just when I really need help.*

She had a large group of six very good divers today, the maximum she could accommodate; four with "advanced" ratings and two certified as "master" divers. Terry did not want her operation to show poorly to this group. At that moment, a young man she had never seen before walked into the marina and came over to her. "Hola, senorita Terry Hunter?"

"Yes, I'm Terry Hunter, how can I help you?"

"My name is Ricky and I am here to help *you*. I am a friend of Pepe's. He had a car accident this morning and called me to assist you." Terry was shocked and concerned for Pepe.

"What happened? Where is he? How is he?"

"He was hit by a car this morning and taken to the hospital." Terry called the hospital on her cell phone and received confirmation that Pepe had been brought in earlier but he was in critical condition and could not talk to her. She had no time to check Ricky's references and she did need the help. She was thankful that Pepe had the presence of mind to get a replacement.

"All right, Ricky, help me load these tanks and equipment aboard.

"OK, Terry, let me check the air level of the tanks first." Ricky opened the air valve of each tank and watched as the air gauge on the regulator registered 3000psi, indicating a full tank. "Terry, this one is low, only 2500psi, I will replace it." A tank that had less than the normal 3000psi is known as a "short-fill." It happens occasionally, and is not a big deal as long as the level is not too low. Still, it's better to have more air than less to start a dive, so the usual procedure is simply to swap the tank for a full one.

Since Terry was already running late, she was going to tell Ricky to ignore it; she would use that short-fill tank. Her breathing underwater was so efficient that she could start a dive with less than a full tank and end the dive with more air than most of the divers who had started with a full tank. Before she could tell Ricky to hook up the short-fill tank to her equipment, he was already walking back from the direction of the tank filling station, near where he had parked his car. "OK, Ricky. Hurry up and get aboard, we have to get going and pick up our divers."

"But I haven't checked the air level of the new tank yet." Terry was impatient now.

"OK, just hook it up to my equipment and check it," she said sharply. Ricky quickly attached Terry's regulator to the new tank and turned on the air valve. Terry watched the needle on the air gauge go to the 3000psi mark, and said, "OK, Manuel, let's shove off and get the hell out of here!"

Terry had been looking forward to today's dives with this group. It was rare that she had an entire group of experienced divers on a single dive.

The fact that she would not have to look after them as closely as novice or less experienced divers, meant that she could spend more of the dive enjoying the marine life around her. The group of divers was staying at a hotel relatively close to the marina, so it was a short ride to pick them up.

Once they were aboard, Manuel headed the *Dorado* out to a reef called Punta Sur, located toward the southern tip of Cozumel, a good 30- to 40-minute ride. Terry relaxed for the first time that day, except for some anxiety about how Pepe was doing at the hospital. The group had requested this location because they wanted a challenging dive. Terry agreed since the certification level of all the divers was sufficient to be able to handle a difficult dive. Moreover, Terry didn't get a chance to dive on this reef very often and she was looking forward to it as much as the others.

Punta Sur offers divers the opportunity to explore a deeper wall than on other reefs. The tops of coral buttresses extend to within 60 feet of the surface, with the best coral, sponges and other marine life at 80 feet or below. The typical dive here is to about 100 feet, approaching the 130-foot depth to which recreational divers are limited. Two major attractions of this dive site are the large, pelagic fish, such as sharks, eagle rays that can be seen here more frequently than at other locations, and a cave and deep tunnel that enables divers to penetrate the wall through a natural formation called The Devil's Throat. Since it requires divers to navigate through a dark passageway without immediate access to the surface, responsible dive operators take only very advanced divers on this dive.

The dive plan was to descend to 80 feet as soon as possible, and explore the wall as they swam towards a cave opening at 95 feet, which led into The Devil's Throat, which would "spit" them out at about 120 feet. Then they would explore the other side of the wall as they slowly ascended to shallower depths and then up to surface after their five-minute safety stop. The total duration would be limited to no more than forty minutes, due to the deep depth of the dive. The excitement and anticipation level among the divers was at a higher intensity level than usual, due to the challenging nature of this dive.

Terry was first to jump in, followed by the rest of the divers. After confirming that everyone was ready, she said, "OK, let's go down!"

Everyone held their inflation/deflation hose above their heads, pressed the "deflate" button and began to descend as the air escaped from their BCs. Terry watched as the group headed toward the sea floor together, trailing a stream of bubbles shimmering like expanding diamonds rising toward the surface. When they reached the sea floor at 80 feet, they began to explore the wonders of the wall: colorful yellow tube sponges, rust-colored barrel sponges and long, thin red rope sponges, formations of star coral and giant brain coral, large schools of jacks, yellow-tail snappers, stripped grunts, and a large grouper just hanging out next to the wall watching curiously as these intruders passed through his world. The divers continued to explore the wall following Terry, and being followed in turn by the curious grouper.

At the 90-foot level, Terry developed a mild headache and felt slightly foggy. She shook her head to clear the cobwebs, distracted by the mild annoyance. At 100 feet she suddenly felt nauseous, something that never happened to her before. *Must have eaten those eggs too fast this morning*, she thought. She continued to feel worse, becoming lightheaded and weak. When the group reached the entrance to The Devil's Throat, the diver behind Terry, Bob Jackson, bumped into her, anticipating that she would continue into the opening. He noticed that she had stopped moving completely and moved around to the front to see what was wrong. He saw that she was unconscious; her regulator was still in her mouth, but just barely.

As a master diver, Jackson was well trained and knew what to do. He immediately clamped his hand over Terry's regulator, keeping it in her mouth so she could continue breathing. Then he put his other arm around her back, grabbed hold of her BC and headed quickly for the surface. The rest of the divers started up, too, but he signaled them to pause and make a controlled ascent.

They had been underwater for about twenty minutes and had reached a depth of 100 feet. Consequently, a rapid ascent could result in a fatal case of decompression sickness. He knew that he had to take the chance in order to save Terry's life, but there was no need to put anyone else in danger. He rapidly continued to the surface, trying not to rise faster than the rate that his bubbles were rising, a visual guideline often used by divers to gauge their rate of ascent, in order to minimize the risk of the bends. Still, he had to eliminate his safety stop and he rose directly to the surface with an unconscious Terry.

"Help us!" he shouted. Manuel and Ricky hauled Terry into the boat, ripped out the regulator from her mouth and began to administer oxygen.

"What happened?" asked Manuel.

"I don't know," Jackson said. "She just fainted and remained unconscious. I brought her up as fast as I could." Even as he spoke he knew that they were both in trouble. He started to feel crippling pain in his right arm and shoulder and when they opened Terry's wet suit they saw that she had developed a rash. These were both symptoms of the bends. Bob started to take some oxygen, as well, as Manuel radioed the hospital to send an ambulance and to prepare the decompression chamber.

A "bent" diver was first recompressed to force the excess nitrogen from his tissues back into solution, and then decompressed slowly while breathing almost pure oxygen, which helped to break down the nitrogen so it could be expelled by the body more easily. Depending on the severity of the situation, a diver could either recover completely, partially with some after-effects, or a diver could die. In this situation, there was the added complication of Terry still being unconscious. *What could have caused that?* they wondered.

The ambulance met the *Dorado* at the marina and took Terry and Bob Jackson to the hospital. There are two decompression chambers available on the island, capable of handling several divers simultaneously. Since Terry's condition appeared to be the worse of the two, she was rushed to the closest chamber, located in a nearby hospital. Bob Jackson preferred to return home, to the United States, so, after an initial decompression treatment, concentrated oxygen was administered to him while he was airlifted to a decompression facility in Miami for further treatment and evaluation.

After the confusion at the dock subsided, Manuel noticed that the tanks, with their equipment still attached, were all lined up in the tank racks on the boat, except for one. Terry's BC and regulator lay on the deck, but the tank to which it had been connected was missing. So was Ricky.

Chapter 20

The next morning, Terry was feeling much better. Although she had indeed suffered a case of decompression illness, it was mild enough that the doctors felt that she would make a complete recovery and be able to resume diving in the near future.

As it turned out, her friend, Doctor Eduardo Sanchez, had been on duty when she was brought in to the emergency area and had supervised her decompression treatment. "You gave us quite a scare, Terry. In fact, if it weren't for the efforts of one of your customers – Bob Jackson, I believe his name was – you most certainly would have drowned. Do you remember exactly what happened?"

"Not too much. I recall feeling like I had a bad headache and then being nauseous. Then I felt some dizziness, and then I don't remember anything else."

"Well, apparently you lost consciousness and senor Jackson realized you were in trouble. He kept your regulator in your mouth so you wouldn't drown and brought you up as quickly as he safely could. Nevertheless you both suffered decompression illness."

"How is he? Is he all right?" Terry asked, genuinely worried about the fate of the diver who had saved her life.

"Yes, he will be fine. He was rushed to Miami for treatment and we have been notified that he is expected to make a full recovery."

"Thank God!" Terry exclaimed. "I sure do owe him a lot. What I can't figure out is what made me sick in the first place. Maybe food poisoning?"

"No, I don't think so," said Doctor Sanchez. "In addition to the rash caused by the decompression illness, your skin had an unusual blush to it, so I had some suspicions about your condition. I ran some blood tests and they confirmed what I thought. You had a high level of carbon monoxide in your blood. That's what gave you the headache, made you nauseous, and eventually resulted in a lack of oxygen to your brain, causing you to black out. It was a case of carbon monoxide poisoning."

Terry thought about this for a few seconds. She knew of rare instances when scuba tanks that were being re-filled had become contaminated because exhaust fumes from a nearby gasoline-powered generator or air pump had seeped into the tank through the filters and mixed with the air.

"Well, I guess that's possible, but the air-filling station that I use is very careful and used well-maintained equipment. I find it hard to believe that an accident like that could have happened."

"One of my fears precisely," said Doctor Sanchez. "Is it possible that it could have been deliberate?"

"Oh, I can't believe that. Who would want to kill me?" But as soon as she said it, Terry thought of one person on Cozumel who hated her enough to do it. Still, why would Oscar take such a chance? She did not want to discuss her history with Dr. Sanchez at this time. "Well, I suppose anything is possible, but I can't think of anyone. I really believe it was just an accident. When can I go home?"

"Tomorrow. I want to give you one more decompression treatment and keep you for observation one more night. One more thing, no diving for three months."

Terry still didn't feel one hundred percent, so she uncharacteristically agreed to being kept in the hospital for one more night. As far as no diving for three months? She would see about that. She couldn't afford not to work for that long, but this wasn't the time to argue about it. "OK, Eduardo, you're the doctor," Terry said cheerfully, to assuage him.

Joe Manetta went to police headquarters to meet with Sergeant Gonzalez after receiving a phone call about Doctor Sanchez' report of the poisoned fish. After he read the report he noticed that someone by the name of Terry Hunter had been copied on the doctor's report. "Why did she get a copy of this report?" asked Manetta, concerned about a security breach.

"I guess it was as a courtesy from Doctor Sanchez. Miss Hunter is a local dive operator. She is the person who found the dead fish and brought them in for analysis."

"I see. Well, I guess my next stop is to visit Doctor Sanchez. Thanks for the report, Sergeant. Please keep me informed of any further developments."

"I will, Detective, good luck."

The next morning, Joe called Doctor Sanchez to introduce himself and to arrange for an appointment. First, he decided to have breakfast in the hotel's outdoor garden restaurant, overlooking the water. He was enjoying the beautiful view, watching the dive boats heading out to the reefs with their dive parties and casually glancing through the morning newspaper when a headline caught his eye: *Two Divers Nearly Die In Diving Accident!* He read on.

> Two experienced divers, Terry Hunter, the owner-operator of *DiveWithTerry* Dive Company, and Bob Jackson, a vacationing diver from the United States, were rushed into decompression treatment following a narrow escape from death...

As he read the rest of the story, something in the back of his mind was nagging him – there was something familiar about one of the names. Suddenly the recollection came to him. Joe took out the copy of the report that Sergeant Gonzalez had given to him. There it was, the same name:

Terry Hunter! The story said that she was in the same hospital where he was scheduled to meet Doctor Sanchez later that morning. *This would be a very interesting meeting*, thought Joe.

Joe arrived at the hospital and discussed the progress of the investigation with Doctor Sanchez, who listened intently. After the doctor had given Joe the conclusions of his analysis, that the fish had been incapacitated and killed by a combination of cocaine and some other toxic substance, Joe asked if he knew anything else about the location where the fish were found. Doctor Sanchez said that, unfortunately, he did not have those details. "Can I question Miss Hunter? I understand that she is still in this hospital."

"Well, she had another decompression treatment last night and she stayed overnight for observation. She is scheduled to be released later today, but we can go up to her room now and see if she can talk with us. She was resting when I checked on her earlier."

They took the elevator to the second floor and went into Terry's room but she appeared to be asleep. Joe was struck by how attractive she was, even while in a hospital bed, without makeup and hooked up to various monitors.

"We better let her rest for now," said Doctor Sanchez. As they turned to leave the room, Joe looked back and muttered softly, "Sleeping like an angel." Terry had been listening to the voices of the two men talking, drifting in and out of the netherworld of the semi-awake. When she heard Joe's comment about an "angel" she cracked one eye half-open and caught a glimpse of his ruggedly handsome profile as he turned to close the door. She dreamily thought to herself, *Did I just go to Heaven?*

Outside Terry's room Doctor Sanchez said, "Perhaps you could be here when Miss Hunter is released. She will need someone to drive her home and you could talk to her then."

"Great idea, Doc. What time should I return?"

"Oh, about 4:00 this afternoon."

"OK, see you then. I think I'll have some lunch and check in with the home office to give them a progress report."

Chapter 21

"I'm sorry, senor, I thought that..." *Smack!*

"Idiot! Shut up!" Oscar roared, as he smashed Ricky across the mouth with the rolled-up newspaper containing the story about Terry Hunter's diving accident.

"But I tried..." *Smack!*

As Ricky was knocked backward, Oscar continued, "I didn't pay you to 'try,' I paid you to kill the bitch, not to give her a fucking headache!"

"It was difficult to get the right amount of fumes into the tank. Too much and she would have gotten sick too soon. If not for that other diver she would be dead right now."

"Excuses! I don't pay for excuses. I pay for performance! Here, I have an easier assignment that you may be able to handle. I have a large group going out with two dive masters in about thirty minutes on the *Santa Rosa II* on a deep wall dive. You go as a third dive master trailing the group in case someone gets into trouble. Do you think you can you handle that?"

"Oh yes, yes," said Ricky, eager to get back in the good graces of his boss.

"One more thing. Take this new BC vest. I am thinking of buying some of these to use as rental equipment. It has integrated weights so we don't have to stock so many separate weight belts. They told me in the equipment shack that you use 6 pounds when you dive, correct?"

"Yes, I am a good diver, sir, I only need six pounds."

"OK, I had them put two 3-pound weights in the weight pockets for you, one on each side. Use it on this dive and let me know how easy it is to use and if you recommend that we purchase a few of them."

"Yes, sir, I will do a good job, I will be very careful to..."

"Get out of my sight!"

Thirty minutes later, Ricky reported dockside to the *Santa Rosa II* with the other two dive masters and helped the divers get on board and set up their equipment. The boat made the trip out to the dive site, the Santa Rosa Reef, which was on the lip of a steep wall. This was to be a deep wall dive, drifting with a moderately strong current. The site was a popular choice for divers, featuring large plate corals, huge sea fans, which swayed gracefully with the current, and an array of colorful sponges. The best diving was along the wall, where divers could explore the marine life as the current moved them along or look into the abyss on the seaward side and imagine they were flying, weightless, thousands of feet above the sea floor. There were also small caves and grottos for the more adventurous divers to explore.

They dropped into the water over the lip of the wall and descended to 60 feet, then began to swim in a gently sloping angle, down toward their planned maximum depth of 90 feet. The tricky part of wall-diving is that, unless you continuously monitor your depth gauge, you could suddenly find that you had descended below your planned depth because there is no sea floor to use as a visual reference. As the large group swam along the wall, the dive was going as planned. As they turned past a protruding outcropping of coral in the wall, Ricky lost sight of the divers ahead of him momentarily as he maintained his position as the last diver in the line.

Descending to 80 feet, Ricky had to transfer some air from his tank to his BC to offset the loss of buoyancy as the additional water pressure at the lower depth compressed his wetsuit. In addition, today's moderately strong current was spilling over the lip of the wall, creating a surge of water called a "downwelling," like an underwater waterfall, which can push a diver deeper. As he reached for the inflator button on his inflation/deflation hose, Ricky felt a tug from behind and he began to sink. He wheeled around, surprised to see another diver, who had looped two 5-pound lead weights onto the air valve on the top of his tank, more than doubling the total weight that Ricky carried, from 6 pounds to 16 pounds. Frantically, he reached behind his neck to remove the additional weight, but it was secured too tightly. Ricky tried to transfer more air to his BC from his air tank, to offset the additional weight by increasing his buoyancy, but the other diver reached forward and pulled the quick-disconnect attachment, separating Ricky's BC inflator hose from his air tank.

Both divers had now sunk to 100 feet, the point where some divers begin to feel the first effects of nitrogen narcosis, the mind-numbing phenomenon that impairs a diver's judgment and ability to think clearly. Many divers know this as "Rapture of the Deep," a term coined by the pioneering "father of scuba diving," Jacques Cousteau. As Ricky fumbled between trying to reattach the air hose to his BC and removing the weights pulling him down, the other diver reached toward him, flipped off Ricky's mask and pulled his regulator out of his mouth, then headed back up to rejoin the group.

Ricky was sufficiently trained to be able to re-insert his regulator, clear it and resume breathing, and also to re-secure his mask and clear the water out of it; all of which he did. But now he was down to 130 feet and sinking faster. He realized his last chance was to ditch his weight belt to restore positive buoyancy, but when he went to release the buckle of the weight belt, it wasn't there. He forgot that this type of BC, which he was using for the first time, had the weights secured inside internal pockets. These weights could be easily ditched, too, but the diver had to remember where the release handles were located.

It wouldn't have mattered, anyway, though. Oscar had secured the pockets with surgical thread. They couldn't be pulled open, but would dissolve in the salt water after a few days, so, in the unlikely event that Ricky's body was ever recovered, he would just appear to be the unfortunate victim of a diving accident, a diver who had been dragged to his death by the current spilling down over a coral wall.

By now, Ricky was at 140 feet and beginning to feel totally euphoric as the rapture of the deep increased in intensity. *Why worry?* he thought to himself as he passed 160 feet. *I have plenty of air to breathe and I can surface later on,* his impaired reasoning told him. He was feeling absolutely giddy as he passed 190 feet. At 200 feet the last thing Ricky ever saw was a large grouper, to whom he tried to give his regulator. *Fish also need air to breathe,* was the last irrational thought that he had, as his body plunged toward the sea floor, 2000 feet below.

Back in his office, Oscar was busy purging the contaminated tank that Ricky had used to try to kill Terry. With Ricky gone, this was the last piece of evidence that could have tied Oscar to the attempt on her life. He couldn't afford any more close calls, especially after having had to bribe the prosecutor to avoid being implicated in the death of Terry's customer two years earlier.

The *Santa Rosa II* returned to the dock a little later, minus one missing dive master. None of the divers had seen what had transpired. So far as they knew, Ricky had been the trailing diver and some accident had befallen him. In a location that featured deep drop-offs and moderately strong currents, this was a rare, but not unheard of, occurrence. There would be a little publicity in the local newspapers, less than if the accident had happened to a wealthy tourist, and only a cursory recovery effort. Oscar would see to it that the recovery effort was even more cursory than usual.

Chapter 22

At four o'clock, Joe Manetta was in the waiting room of the hospital when Doctor Sanchez summoned him up to Terry's room.

When Joe walked into the room, Doctor Sanchez introduced him to Terry. "Terry, this is Detective Joseph Manetta, a friend from the New York City Police Department. He has generously offered to give you a ride home."

Terry immediately recognized him as the man whose profile she had seen leaving her room yesterday. *Hmm, not too bad up close*, she thought. Terry smiled as she extended her hand, "Nice to meet you, Detective Manetta. Eduardo, I am *very* impressed that you arranged a police escort for me, all the way from the Big Apple, too." They all laughed at Terry's good-natured teasing of the New York detective.

Joe was trained to be able to read people, and when Terry had moved forward to shake his hand, he read a look of recognition in her face, but how? She had been sleeping when he had been in her room yesterday and he was sure they had never met before. He thought, *I would surely remember having met this lady before!* Seeing her now, standing in front of him, not lying in bed in hospital garb, but dressed in jeans and a snug-fitting blouse, he was even more impressed. Joe was a well proportioned six-footer and Terry was only a couple of inches shorter, even only wearing sneakers. He also noticed that she looked remarkably fit and toned, even after a stay in the hospital. *Well, makes sense, she does swim and dive every day,* he reasoned.

"Shall we go?" Doctor Sanchez suggested.

"OK, but first I want to see how Pepe is doing. I haven't had a chance to see him since my accident."

"Pepe?" Joe asked.

"Yes, he's my boatmate. On the day of my accident he was hit by a car and is in critical condition. I really want to see how he's feeling."

Joe's investigative instincts kicked in. "So he wasn't on the boat with you the day of your accident?"

"No, but he arranged for a substitute so I wouldn't be short-handed. Wasn't that thoughtful of him?"

"Yes, it was," Joe remarked, processing this bit of information, like a piece of a puzzle that didn't exactly fit right in his mind. As they went to Pepe's room they saw that he was in traction and semi-conscious due to heavy sedation.

The duty nurse said, "He has two broken legs and a shattered pelvis, but he is more stable today and we expect him to survive. We still do not know how many operations will be required to enable him to walk again."

Joe commented to the nurse, "I guess he was in pretty bad shape when they brought him in."

"Yes, critical condition. We really didn't expect him to live, but he is young and strong. That's what saved his life."

By the time Terry and Joe left the hospital it was after 5 o'clock. Joe said, "Ms. Hunter, I know it's a bit early, but do you feel like having some dinner?"

"You bet, and you can call me Terry. I'm famished after eating hospital food for two days. I could eat a horse! I know just the place."

"Oh, you mean that stable we passed a mile back?"

Terry laughed, *OK, so he has a sense of humor*. "No, there's a place in town that is one of my favorites. Make a left at the next corner."

"Yes, ma'am."

"Just what I like," she said laughing, "a man who knows who's the boss."

Ten minutes later they parked in front of Pancho's Backyard. As they went in, Terry noticed that Joe was eyeballing the t-shirts in the front section of the building. "Looking for a souvenir for someone?"

"No, just looking," said Joe, thinking about the lack of success he had been having with his current, 'drugs-in-the-t-shirt' smuggling theory. They sat down at a quiet table in a corner, screened by palm shrubs. "Nice choice, good place for a romantic date."

"The food's good, too," said Terry. They ordered margaritas, on the rocks with salt, while they scanned their menus. The waiter came by and asked if they needed more time. Joe nodded toward Terry, who said, "I know what I'm having. The broiled lobster tails over rice."

"The barbecued shrimp look good, I'll try that."

"That's a good choice," said Terry. "They serve the shrimp on a skewer, over hot coals. One of my favorites."

They relaxed and snacked on chips waiting for their drinks. "So how do you know Eduardo?" Terry asked.

"Well, I'm in Cozumel on official business and I saw his name in a report concerning a matter that I'm investigating. In fact, your name is also in the report, so I have to ask you some questions."

"So we are here on official business?" Terry asked, genuinely surprised.

"Well, sort of." Terry leaned across the table, resting her chin in her hands and looked straight into Joe's eyes.

"And what if I refuse to answer your questions, mister detective?" Terry couldn't hide the mischievous gleam in her eyes. Joe read it and decided to have some fun of his own.

"Then I may have to lock you up. You know, in protective custody, for your own safety."

"For how long?"

"Indefinitely, until you cooperate with us."

"Is that any way to treat an *angel?*" Terry said, with the emphasis on the word "angel."

Joe was caught totally off-guard and stammered, as Terry thought, *gotcha, wise guy!*

"But how did you... when did you... you were asleep when I said that!"

"And you call yourself a detective!" Terry said dismissively, rolling her eyes in mock disrespect.

"Why, you little devil!"

"Me? I'm an '*angel.*' You said so yourself."

"The Devil in disguise!"

"Elvis Presley, 1963! Great song."

They both laughed, as Joe put his arms up, palms forward in a comic gesture of surrender. He then pantomimed writing in an imaginary notebook, "OK, you're ahead, Terry 3, Joe 1." Terry continued to laugh, appreciating the fact that Joe could take a joke. She thought to herself, *I haven't had so much fun sparring with someone since, since, well, since Mark and I...* Joe caught the change in her eyes, from a funny twinkle to a sad distance. "Hey, you OK?"

"Yes," Terry said as she came back to the present, "Just a quick visit to a past memory."

"I get those, too, sometimes." Joe said, with a warm but sad smile, which touched Terry and increased her curiosity about Joe. "Was your past memory a husband?"

"No, close once, though. How about you? Were you ever married?"

"Yes. Was once, but not now."

Both sensed that the other did not want to reveal any more about their past, so after a moment of awkward silence, Terry switched conversational gears. "So, what about this investigation of yours, how does it involve me?"

"We're investigating a drug smuggling operation, cocaine specifically. We believe we have narrowed the possible sources down to a few islands in the Caribbean; Cozumel is one of them."

"How am I involved?"

"I saw your name in the report that Doctor Sanchez sent to the police and then I saw your name in the paper about your near-death experience. I thought there might be a connection."

"But that was an accident!"

"Listen, Terry, I don't think so. You may have stumbled into more than you realize and someone may be trying to silence you."

"Oh, come on, now. You don't really..." Terry broke off in mid-sentence, recalling that Doctor Sanchez had also mentioned that he had a similar suspicion.

"OK, who was that replacement who conveniently showed up the day of Pepe's accident?"

"I don't know exactly who he is; he said his name is Ricky. He's a friend of Pepe, he just came because Pepe called him."

"Really? And how did Pepe call him from the hospital in critical condition? Where is he now?"

"I was so busy that day I never thought about it. I don't know where he is. I haven't seen or heard from him since the accident. Wait a minute!" Terry said, as she connected the dots that Joe had laid out. "How did he know to show up, that Pepe would be in an accident, unless... "

"Unless?"

"Unless Pepe's 'accident' was no accident, either!"

"Precisely, Dr. Watson."

"Oh my God!" Terry said, as a shiver ran down her spine.

"I sure would like to talk to this 'Ricky' character. Any ideas about how I can get in touch with him or anyone who knows him?'

"No, but tonight I'll call my boat captain, Manuel. He knows just about everyone on Cozumel."

"Well, that's a start. Looks like the food's here. How about a bottle of wine with dinner?"

"Right now I could down a bottle myself."

As the waiter served the meal, Joe said, "Could we see a wine list, please?"

The evening progressed, and Terry and Joe found that they enjoyed being in each other's company, as the conversation flowed at a relaxing but interesting pace. Terry exuded a sense of confidence and zest for life that Joe found uplifting. After Mark's death, Terry had not dated anyone for over a year. When she had finally decided that she was ready to start meeting people again, there was no shortage of available men, but she discovered that no one could come close to the standard that Mark had set. So she had dated occasionally, but no one could really connect with her soul.

Terry felt that Joe Manetta was different, somehow, though she couldn't put her finger on it. Sure, he was ruggedly handsome, but there was more. He seemed well grounded, had a good sense about himself, self-assuredness, a sense of depth that Terry found intriguing.

Joe had not felt much emotion for anyone since he had lost Jenny three years ago. His buddies had fixed him up with some dates, trying to get their friend "back in the saddle," in a supportive way. But for Joe, it just wasn't the same. Tonight, however, he felt protective toward Terry in a way that he had not felt toward anyone for three years, despite the strong sense of independence that she projected. He was starting to feel other emotions that had been strangers to him for three years. *Get hold of yourself,* he thought, *this wine must be stronger than I thought.* "May I get either of you coffee or dessert?"

"I'll just have coffee," Joe said to the waiter. "How about you?"

"Sounds good, but what do you have for dessert?" As Joe smiled at her, Terry leaned across the table and said in a loud whisper, "Well, I *do* have to get my strength back, you know!"

After coffee and dessert, while Joe was paying the check, Terry teased him. "Make sure you leave a good tip, I have my reputation to maintain."

"Just what I needed, a date with the last of the big-time spenders."

"This wasn't a date, Detective Manetta. This was an official interrogation."

"Hey," he said, examining her arm, "look, no bruises, and I never even took out the rubber hose."

They laughed as they walked to Joe's car. Joe opened the door and, as he held Terry's hand for a brief moment to help her into the car, he felt the warmth and softness of her skin. The small gesture felt so comfortable, so natural, so *good,* that he was unsettled for a moment. As he walked around to the driver's side of the car he ran his hand through his hair, trying to clear his mind, confused by what he was feeling.

The ride back to Terry's apartment was only fifteen minutes. It was only 9 o'clock but Terry was exhausted. Her stay in the hospital, and the realization during her conversation with Joe that someone had actually tried to kill her, had left her physically and emotionally drained.

"Well, thanks for dinner, Detective Manetta," Terry said, extending her hand and forcing a smile. "It really was a very pleasant evening, despite the fact that you convinced me that I'm a target." Joe shook her hand, silently admiring her poise. Before he could open his door to help Terry, she was already out of the car.

"Wait a minute," he called to her, quickly writing the phone number of his hotel on his business card. "Here's my number. Call me if you need anything, if something happens, anything at all."

"Thanks. After I talk to Manuel I'll call you and let you know what I find out about Ricky. Good night and thanks again, Joe. I really did have a nice time tonight." Joe watched her go into her apartment building and up the stairs to the second floor. He looked around to be sure that Terry had not been followed and then drove back to his hotel. He was surprised how quickly he arrived at his hotel, and then realized that his mind had been on Terry Hunter, not his driving.

He went to his room and decided to write some reports to send back to task force headquarters but he had difficulty concentrating. He shook his head to clear it and started to write but his mind kept reflecting back on the evening, the delicious dinner, the pleasant company and enjoyable conversation. *Get a hold of yourself, Joe, old boy. You have a job to do, so focus!*

Back in her apartment, Terry rested on the bed for a moment before calling Manuel, but found herself thinking about the evening she had spent with Detective Manetta. She needed to close her eyes, just for a moment. When the sunlight streaming through her window woke her up, Terry realized she had slept until the next afternoon. "Damn," she exclaimed to herself. She tried calling Manuel, but when he did not answer she realized he was either at the marina working on the *Dorado* or already out on the water with a charter group. She decided to do some chores around the apartment and call Manuel later.

Several hours later, when she was about to call again, she saw Joe's number on his business card and decided to call him. She received no answer because Joe was in the business office of the hotel faxing reports to Miami so she left a voice mail message. When Joe returned in the early evening, he returned her call. "Hi, Terry, I got your message. What's up? Anything wrong?"

"Oh, no. I never got to call Manuel last night. I was going to call him now and see if he knows anything about Ricky, but I was just wondering if you would want to be here when I do. If he does know anything about Ricky, you may want to ask him some questions immediately."

"Sure, does he speak English? My Spanish isn't the best."

"Oh yes, he speaks English. He had a great teacher. I'll tell you all about that story sometime."

"OK. I want to grab a quick bite first. I'll be over in about an hour. See you then." Joe arrived at Terry's apartment at about 8:00pm. Her apartment was cozy, a three-room, second floor walk-up with a living room, kitchen with dinette area and a bedroom. As an added touch there was a sun porch that actually was the roof of a downstairs room. "Nice place you have."

"Thanks. Not very fancy, but I like it. Let me call Manuel, I don't want to keep you here any longer than you want to."

"That's OK, all I have to worry about is getting out the next report to my boss in New York. He wants to make sure I'm not having too much fun."

"Hello, Manuel, it's Terry. How are you? Yes, I'm fine I just got home from the hospital yesterday. Manuel, I have to find out something; it's very important. Do you know anything about Ricky? Have you seen him, or..."

Manuel interrupted Terry's questioning and she fell silent. Joe watched her closely while Manuel was speaking, telling Terry all he had learned about Ricky. Joe watched her body language change and stepped toward her as he became concerned that whatever Manuel was telling her about Ricky was upsetting her. She was gripping the receiver of the phone with two hands so hard that her knuckles were turning white and her shoulders were beginning to shake.

Terry didn't notice that Joe was standing behind her holding her shoulders to steady her; in fact, she hadn't even heard what Manuel was saying for the past few seconds, not after he had heard him say, "...works for Oscar!" She let the phone fall to the floor and sagged against Joe. He helped her to a chair and put the phone back on its cradle. He turned to see her holding her head in her hands, repeating the words, "No, not Oscar again. Not Oscar again."

Joe got Terry a glass of water and asked her, "OK, what about Oscar?" Terry composed herself and told him the whole history between her and Oscar. She felt better having talked it through. Just having someone listen to her was therapeutic.

Terry stood up a few minutes later and walked toward the window, looking more like herself again. Looking out toward the West, one could just barely make out the glow in the sky from the lights of the resorts on the mainland, just across the channel. "Pretty, isn't it?" she said. Joe walked over and stood behind her. "Beautiful" was all he said and Terry could feel his breath on the back of her neck when he spoke. She turned to face him, and they looked at each other, eyes only inches apart.

"Joe, I... " Suddenly, Joe took her in his arms and kissed her, passionately on her lips. Terry did not draw away but held him tightly. After a minute, Joe stepped back and looked at Terry. "Terry," he stammered, "I'm so sorry, that was unprofessional of me, I didn't mean to ...." She stepped toward him and pulled him closer, kissing his cheek and, as she put her hand behind his neck, gently pulling his head close to her, she whispered in his ear, "That's OK, Joe. It's all right."
And then Joe looked into her eyes, caressed her face with his hand and kissed her again.

They never made it to the bedroom only a few steps away, collapsing instead onto the sofa in the living room. The years of pain and frustration they had both endured exploded into a frenzy of passion. Joe was amazed at the incredible intensity of Terry's lovemaking. She was insatiable, and he had never before experienced anything like the level of pleasure that she gave him.

Terry thoroughly enjoyed the way that Joe made love to her, a combination of sensitivity and tenderness, coupled with his own fierce desire. She allowed herself to surrender and simply enjoy sensation after sensation. Several orgasms later, she was a very satisfied lady, and, as the last waves of pleasure swept through her body, she held him tightly against her, almost as if she were afraid to let go.

After a few peaceful moments, Terry looked over at Joe and dreamily said, "I don't think you're in any condition to drive home tonight, Detective Manetta."

He answered in a wearily husky voice. "No, not in any condition, not in any shape, not in any way! How's the breakfast service in this establishment?"

"I hear the chef cooks up the best omelet you ever ate."

"OK, see you in the morning," he said, nuzzling her ear.

Chapter 23

Oscar was standing on the shore, at a deserted part of the island about two miles south of the Playa Divers pier. He was holding a lantern, shielded to throw a narrow beam of light in a single direction, in order to avoid detection. Soon, an approaching boat that he could hear, but not yet see, flashed a light toward him, in a sequence of three flashes, two flashes, and one flash. Oscar answered back with the opposite pattern: one flash, two flashes, and three flashes.

The boat proceeded toward shore, satisfied that the pre-determined code had been confirmed. Oscar and three of his partners walked out into the water to meet the boat until they were waist-deep, each towing a small raft. Oscar took a large pouch from his raft and gave it to the captain of the boat, who checked the contents. In the darkness, Oscar could hear metallic clicking sound of automatic weapons being readied to fire. Satisfied that the pouch contained the agreed-upon sum of money, the captain nodded to the boat crew, who put their weapons down and started to load plastic bags containing a white powdered substance onto the four rafts.

The transaction complete, the boat began to back away, while Oscar and his men towed the heavily laden rafts toward the shore. Not a word had been exchanged during the entire transaction.

Back on shore, the men transferred the contents from the rafts to the back of Oscar's pick-up truck and stacked the rafts on top. They drove for several miles around the southern tip of Cozumel to the more deserted eastern side of the island, which faced the pounding of the heavy surf of the open ocean. They parked the truck behind a small concrete building, not much bigger than a shack, and brought the bags of white powder inside, along with several other smaller bags containing a brown granular substance that Oscar had brought with him.

"Let's get to work quickly," Oscar said, "The *Sea Queen* will be docking downtown in two days. We must have this shipment ready to be picked up by then."

Each man knew his job, so conversation was held to a minimum. First the powder, about 20 kilos at a time, was mixed with distilled water in a large vat. It was not fully diluted, but mixed to a pasty consistency. Then the brown substance was added, carefully, a little at a time, until the mixture became a little firmer. The mixture was stirred with large wooden paddles for several minutes. While the mixture was being stirred, molds were set along a long bench. The bench was about 25 feet long, containing a row of about 20 molds. When the mixture was deemed ready for the next step, the vat was attached to a roller on an overhead rail running several feet over the bench.

Then the vat was rolled along, stopping over each mold, where one of the gang would open a small valve, letting the mixture of cocaine fill each mold before closing the valve and moving on to the next one. Small gutters alongside the bench caught the waste, which was poured back into the vat. After each pass of the bench, 20 new molds were set up and the process was completed until the entire several-hundred-kilo shipment of cocaine was cast into molds, made to resemble various types of coral: brain coral, star coral, elkhorn and staghorn coral.

The brown substance being mixed in with the cocaine was a specially formulated, industrial strength, waterproof glue, which enabled the cocaine to hold the shape of the coral cast. Oscar had ordered the glue from a local manufacturer, who had no reason to question what seemed to be a legitimate business order. The plan to disguise the cocaine in the form of coral had sprung into Oscar's mind one day as he was watching customers purchase simulated coral souvenirs in the Playa Divers gift shop outside of his office. A tourist asked, "Any problems bringing this coral through U.S. Customs?"

"On no," said the clerk behind the sales counter. "This is only imitation coral. Many countries ban you from bringing in real coral, but this is no problem."

The idea struck Oscar like a thunderbolt. He had been a small-time drug smuggler for several years, exporting a few kilos of heroin or cocaine at a time to the United States. U.S. Customs performed only cursory checks on travelers coming back from Cozumel, usually laden down with dive gear. Consequently, Oscar's drug runners had consistently made it through successfully. He benefited from the fact that Cozumel was known primarily as a diver's paradise, not a major drug-importation route.

Increasing the frequency and size of the shipments required a new approach, however. Oscar had racked his cunning mind for months, trying to find a new angle, and now it had just come to him in a flash of accidental inspiration.

But Oscar had even larger aspirations – he wanted to be a major player, make a big score, lots of big scores; but how? Getting the drugs out of Cozumel was only half of the problem. To realize his dreams he would have to be able to distribute his drugs over a wide area. He had already made contacts that could ensure distribution up the eastern coast of the United States, right into the lucrative New York City area, but he needed a transportation network into the Midwest and West, through the heartland of the United States.

One day a couple of summers earlier, he had struck up a casual conversation with a tourist who was returning some rental equipment after coming off one of his boats on the last dive of his vacation. Oscar learned that the tourist owned his own small trucking company, based in the Midwest, and was planning to expand into the South. Oscar had an uncanny knack for reading people. It was one of his strengths that had served him well in his dealings with thugs, drug dealers and murderers, as well as legitimate business people. He could spot a weakness in someone's character and exploit it to his advantage, or avoid what could be a dangerous situation if his prospect proved to be someone who could ultimately hurt him. He believed, rightfully so, that this skill had probably saved his life on at least one occasion.

The flaw that he had sensed in the character of this hapless tourist was greed and a willingness to use any means to achieve his ambitions. "Come into my office for a drink, amigo," the spider said to the oblivious fly. "It's the least I can do for one of my best customers before you return home." By the time Oscar had finished spinning his web of seduction and deceit by appealing to the businessman's ego and lust for a better life, he had succeeded in securing an agreement from him to transport his cocaine from Miami into the Midwest region of the U.S.

The businessman thought that would be the end of his involvement, but Oscar had other long-range plans. He knew that once he had this new route in place it would be an easy play to convince this naïve sucker, by flattery, blackmail or other means, to expand the transportation network through to the West Coast. No, Carl Olsen had no idea just who he was dealing with.

After the evening's operation was completed, the simulated coral castings were set out on the floor of the concrete building under a bank of heat lamps, to dry overnight. The entire process was completed by about 3 o'clock in the morning. Oscar and one of his partners left, leaving the other two men behind to guard the cocaine as it dried and hardened. Later the next day, the two men would pack the dried cocaine "coral" into waterproof boxes, each holding 20 coral casts, each casting weighing about 1 kilo, and then wait for Oscar to return.

Chapter 24

"My compliments to the chef," said Joe the next morning. "You were right. This is the best omelet I've had in a long time."

"I'll pass your compliments along," said Terry, walking out of the kitchen and gently kissing Joe on the head as she handed him a cup of hot coffee and sat down to join him for breakfast.

They looked at each other for a few seconds and then Terry spoke first. "Joe, last night, well, that was not my usual behavior. I don't just meet a guy one day and the next day ask him to come up and stay the night." Joe just watched Terry and listened. "But I have to tell you, it sure was an incredible evening, I mean, well, how do I say this? I felt that there was a connection, you know, I mean, oh hell, I'm never this inarticulate!" Joe smiled.

"I think I know what you mean, Terry. I felt it, too. I didn't expect last night to happen the way it did, either, but I can't say that I'm sorry about it."

"Me, neither. Quite honestly, I felt that I was connecting with you in a way that I haven't with anyone else, for many years." Joe watched her eyes and saw the same sad, distant look that he saw in the restaurant the other night.

"With the same person that you said you were close to marrying?"

"Yes." Joe saw the tears welling up in Terry's eyes. "I don't think I can ever forget him."

"You shouldn't have to, Terry."

"But after last night I feel that it's somehow all right, almost as if I have permission to move on. Oh, I don't mean to make you feel responsible or anything like that, Joe. It's something I have to work out."

"It's OK, Terry. I know what you mean, what it feels like to want to move on, but almost feeling guilty because you want to." Terry looked at Joe closely and saw him blink back a tear.

"Was it difficult for you after your divorce?" Joe hesitated for a moment and then took a deep breath.

"There was no divorce. Several years ago, Jenny, my wife, was killed in an automobile accident by a couple of guys who were high on drugs." Terry was stunned, not expecting to hear what she had just been told. She reached across the table and put her hand on top of Joe's. "My twin boys, Bobby and Andy, three years old, were also killed, and Jenny was expecting our third child. She was four months pregnant."

Joe looked down at the table, but this time he couldn't blink back the tears. Terry squeezed Joe's hand tightly and, as she moved and knelt beside him, she put her arm around his shoulders. Joe rested his head against Terry's chest and, as she pressed his head against her, she felt him sobbing softly.

A few minutes later they both stood up and walked over to the window, holding hands. They looked out toward the distant water and then at each other. Joe simply said, "Thank you."

Terry said, "Let's go inside." There was nothing else to say. They made love for several hours, but not with the same fierce passion of the night before. This time, they were just there for each other, to give what the other needed.

After lunch, Joe said, "Terry, I wish I could stay longer, but I have to get back to my hotel and fire off a report to my boss. I'm late and I have a lot to tell him."

"Just how much *are* you going to tell him?" asked Terry, in a seductive tone.

"Just enough to keep him off my butt – and just about business," Joe said as he laughed. "Which reminds me, we never did get to talk about my investigation last night. I have a lot of things to ask you. How 'bout I call you and we meet later and go over this stuff?"

"Throw in dinner and it's a deal."

"Deal. What are you doing for the rest of the day?"

"Oh, I thought I might go for a dip and see what's going on."

"I thought that you were supposed to keep away from diving for a couple of months after a decompression situation like you had."

"Well, it's already been a week and I feel fine. This is the longest I've been out of the water in almost a year. I feel like my gills are drying up. I won't do a very long dive and I'll stay shallow, nothing adventurous. I just want to check on a few things."

"Looks to me like you plan on starting your own personal investigation. That's not a good idea, especially with people already trying to kill you."

"I guess you're right. Don't worry; I won't go off half-cocked on my own mission. But I just can't sit still and do nothing, Joe! That's not me. I'm damned angry that someone, well not just someone, but a particular someone, tried to kill me."

"OK, Terry. Look, just be careful. If you're going to dive, stay away from the area where you found those dead fish. The fact that you found those fish in that location seems to have struck a nerve in someone."

Terry didn't respond, because she didn't want to lie to Joe and she didn't want to fight with him, because that's exactly where she planned to dive. "I have to go; see you later." They kissed goodbye, in the way that new lovers kiss at every occasion in a new relationship.

After he finished his report to New York and to the task force headquarters, Joe went to the police station to inform Sergeant Gonzalez about what he had learned about Ricky. He had built a good rapport with the sergeant, based on trust and two-way communication, and he did not want to jeopardize the relationship. No matter what language they speak, police the world over have a common bond in the way they are trained to think. When Joe laid out the sequence of events as he saw it, from Pepe's accident, to Ricky suddenly showing up to offer his services, to the fact that he was known to work for Oscar, Sergeant Gonzalez was just as capable as Detective Joe Manetta in connecting the dots. "I think we should pay an official visit to Senor Oscar."

"My thoughts exactly, Sergeant." Just before the two men left for Playa Divers, a phone call was made from the police station and the phone on Oscar's desk rang. When they arrived twenty minutes later, they were informed that Oscar had left a few minutes earlier, but no one seemed to know for where or when he would return.

There seemed to be a commotion out on the pier so they walked out to see what was happening. Divers were frantically loading dive boats with tanks and equipment and heading out with dive masters, but no customers. "What's going on here?" asked Sergeant Gonzalez.

"Haven't you heard, sir? There has been a horrible accident! Ricky, one of our dive masters, was lost yesterday on a group dive. By now he must be presumed to be dead but we are still looking for him."

Joe turned to Sergeant Gonzalez and said, "Too many accidents happen on this island, if you ask me, Sergeant."

Chapter 25

Later that same afternoon, Oscar and his partner stopped at the shed to see if the packing was completed. "Hurry up! This has to be finished so we can make the drop by tonight and our friends can make their pickup tomorrow night." The usual procedure was for Oscar and his partners to drop off the boxes at a pre-arranged location, after which, accomplices working on the cruise ship would retrieve them. For security purposes, there would be no face-to-face transfer of the cocaine. This would minimize the chance that the entire ring would be broken in the event that the police had one group under surveillance.

After the transaction was completed, Oscar would call his offshore bank, usually the next day, to confirm that payment had been made to his account. Although this delivery method entailed the risk of not being paid for a shipment, it was only a one-time risk, well worth it for the additional safety. Besides, welching on a drug deal was not good for a long-term profitable business relationship, and usually had fatal consequences.

Once transferred to the *Sea Queen*, the cocaine "coral" casts would be stored aboard for the return trip to Miami, appearing to be unsold souvenir items. Accomplices aboard the ship would adjust the ship's manifest so that the unsold coral casts showed up as part of the ship's inventory. The fact that the coral was not genuine made the entire smuggling operation easier because, for environmental and conservational reasons, there was a ban on harvesting and selling real coral. It was, however, perfectly legal to sell simulated coral. The "unsold souvenirs" would be off-loaded and stored in the cruise line's warehouse, supposedly to be loaded onto another outgoing cruise ship for sale to passengers.

Of course, the coral casts would disappear long before the next ship was ready to sail. They were moved to a processing shop, located in the basement of the warehouse, where the casts were ground down back into powder, and loaded onto trucks bound for New York and St. Louis. Unfortunately for the users, the glue was also ground down with the cocaine. It was simply too much trouble to separate it from the cocaine, and the suppliers were unaware that it was poisonous when ingested.

The two men at the shed finished packing the last of the cocaine and Oscar and his partner inspected it. "Good job, nice and tight. Not like the last time when that idiot Chico left a corner open and it split open under water." The men looked at each other with relieved looks on their faces. No one had seen Chico after that accident and no one asked any questions about what had happened to him. Oscar's explosive temper was legendary.

"OK, you three will meet here tonight at 9 o'clock, load everything into the truck and bring it to the beach by 10 o'clock. I'll have the diving equipment with me on the boat and we will deliver our shipment. Any questions?" No one had to ask any questions; they had all done this before, but Oscar liked to go over the plan each time, just to be sure there would be no surprises. Oscar hated surprises.

Chapter 26

Terry called Manuel and told him to meet her at the marina. After overcoming his objections about diving so soon after her "accident," she told him to bring the *Dorado* to the dock in an hour. He was already waiting for her on the dock when she arrived and they greeted each other warmly. "You know you are like a daughter to me. I would die if anything happened to you." Terry kissed him on the cheek.

"Thank you, Manuel, that means so much to me. And thank you for finding out about Ricky's connection to Oscar. That really filled in a lot of the puzzle. I think Joe and Sergeant Gonzalez went to find him today for questioning."

"Didn't you hear the news?"

"No. What?"

"Ricky was lost on a deep dive at Santa Rosa Reef yesterday. They presume that he drowned, but they have not found his body yet."

Terry was surprised but not shocked. Very little shocked her anymore. "Son-of-a-bitch doesn't leave any loose ends, does he?" she said.

"You mean..."

"Yeah, Oscar. Well, let's go diving," Terry said, trying to mask her feelings of vulnerability and anxiety over what Oscar's next move might be.

"Where are you planning to go? I am afraid to ask."

"You're right, Manuel. We're going to the wreck to look around some more. I don't want to attract any attention, though, so don't moor up to the buoy. Drop me off over Chankanaab Reef and I'll drift-dive my way over to the wreck. If the current is strong today, I should be able to cover a lot of ground if I just relax and let the current carry me. Just let the boat drift with the current past the wreck and wait for me about a half a mile away. I don't plan on being under for more than forty-five minutes, so after about thirty-five or forty minutes start looking for me when I inflate my bright orange safety-sausage."

As Terry prepared to roll into the water she looked over at Chankanaab National Park and at the adjoining captive dolphin facility. It had been set up supposedly to study dolphins, but in reality it was just a moneymaker – a very good moneymaker. Tourists paid over one hundred dollars for the privilege of swimming with a dolphin for about an hour. Terry didn't know what the dolphins got out of it. Was the "fun" of playing with a human worth the price of the loss of their freedom? Terry doubted it.

She indicated to Manuel that she was all right and she began her descent. Chankanaab reef was full of life today. Just looking around as she descended, she saw large schools of yellow-striped grunts, several large barracuda, a large southern sting ray and, sleeping under a ledge, a large nurse shark. *Too bad I have no customers on this dive*, she thought, *would have gotten some big tips.* The tips always seemed to flow more freely when the customers had an especially exciting dive and saw a lot of interesting things.

The current was strong today, so Terry could just relax, fold her arms and take in the passing scenery as she moved along with the current. She looked over her shoulder and noticed a small, hawksbill turtle keeping pace just behind her. Suddenly there was a fleeting shadow, then another. By the time she turned to look for them they were gone. Then, as she felt a strange vibration through her mid-section – they came in from a different angle and were on her. Notchka and Lucky! She realized that they had been scanning her with their echolocation sonar, causing the vibrations that she felt. *I wonder what I look like inside to them?*

She welcomed them with arms held wide and they allowed her to stroke their bellies as they passed. They were in a mood to play. Terry had been seeing them more frequently in this vicinity lately, but didn't know why. Then she put it all together. Their appearances had been more frequent since the captive dolphin facility had been built. The captive dolphins were probably from their main pod, maybe even relatives, cousins or siblings. Dolphins are social animals and can communicate with each other over long distances, using their ability to generate a wide range of sounds, whistles and clicks in their own language.

The dolphin facility was separated from the open water only by chain link fencing and netting, constructed in such a way that the dolphins were kept in, but fresh sea water, and hence, sound, were able to pass through easily. *They must be coming around to visit their captive friends,* Terry thought. After a few more playful passes they left as quickly as they appeared. *Oh well, I have work to do, anyway, no time to play.*

In a few more minutes the current brought Terry over the wreck. She didn't want to dive to the bottom, 80 feet below, on this first dive, so she held onto part of the ship's superstructure at about 40 feet and looked around. Everything appeared normal, but wait, what was that? Several fish were swimming around one of the open hatches on the deck in strange circles, some sideways, a couple upside-down.

She let go of her handhold and drifted toward the stern and, looking down, saw some dead fish in the sand near the coral-encrusted propellers and rudder being eaten by scavengers, crabs and mollusks. Terry kicked against the current for a few minutes to hold her position and to look for some more evidence that there was something wrong here. After several minutes she began to tire, so she let the current take her, looking backward at the wreck as she drifted away.

Terry looked at the readout on the dive computer on her wrist. Dive time, 30 minutes; maximum depth, 45 feet; current depth, 35 feet. *OK, this has been long enough,* she figured. As she continued to drift, she began a gradual ascent to fifteen feet, the depth she would hold as she continued to drift for another five minutes before surfacing. Manuel followed her bubbles and, when she surfaced, the *Dorado* was only twenty yards away. After Manuel helped her aboard he asked, "What did you find?"

"Nothing new really, just more sick and dead fish. I haven't seen sick fish anywhere else on the reefs, so clearly something in this area is affecting them. Let's head back in." As they tied the boat up to the dock, Joe and Sergeant Sanchez drove into the marina. "How was the diving today?" Joe asked Terry.

"Fine, good to be back in the water again." She said as she began unloading her equipment.

"Here, let me help you with that."

"Thanks."

"See anything interesting?"

"Just a few more sick fish around the wreck," Manuel offered, trying to be helpful.

"What?! Terry, you said you wouldn't dive near there!" Joe exclaimed, extremely upset. Terry shot Manuel a glance that said more than *Shut up*, and he immediately realized he had said too much.

"Well, I never said anything about where I was going to dive. Besides, Manuel dropped me off over at Chankanaab Reef, some distance away. I can't help it if the current took me in that direction."

"Oh, Terry, what a lame story. You don't... oh never mind." Joe said, not wanting to argue with Terry in front of Manuel and Sergeant Gonzalez. "Let's get some dinner. Thanks for the lift, Sergeant; I'll drive back with Terry. I'll call you tomorrow."

As Sergeant Gonzalez got into his car, he turned to Joe. "I think we have worked together long enough that we can eliminate the formalities, Joe. Why not just call me Rafael?"

"Ok, thanks Rafael, I'd like that, too; talk to you tomorrow."

Terry drove Joe back to her apartment. They went upstairs and Joe sat down in the kitchen to relax as Terry turned on the shower. As she stepped into the shower she called out to Joe, "Hey, Detective, got a minute?"

Joe poked his head into the bathroom and Terry pulled back the shower curtain half-way. "You look like you've had a hot day, why don't you jump in and freshen up? I may even let you frisk me." That was an invitation Joe couldn't pass up. As they soaped up and began to explore each other's bodies, Joe quickly forgot about how angry he had been at Terry's deception about her dive plans. Terry leaned back against Joe and enjoyed feeling secure as he enveloped her in his strong arms. He held her tightly and as he kissed her neck, she closed her eyes and relaxed, letting her sense of vulnerability melt away.

After a long, sensual shower, they dressed for dinner and drove into town, to Santiago's Grill, another of Terry's favorite restaurants. Terry parked a couple of blocks away and they held hands as they walked slowly to the restaurant, enjoying the breezy night air and the salt-smell of the sea.

After ordering drinks, Joe said, "Terry, I've been thinking. How about letting me dive with you to investigate what looks like a link between your dead fish and possibly the drugs I am looking for. From what Manuel so conveniently said today, I assume you first found the fish that you brought to Doctor Sanchez near some wreck, probably where you went diving today."

"Yes, when I was diving on the wreck of the *Felipe Xicotencatl.* It's an old minesweeper, intentionally sunk a year or so ago by the government in order to give divers something interesting on which to dive and to attract fish as it becomes encrusted with coral. It's lying in about 80 feet of water, near the Chankanaab Reef. Most of the sick fish that I've seen have been hanging around the stern, either just outside by the prop and rudder or swimming around one of the open hatches on the deck.

"Sounds like something must be deep inside. Could there be any pollutants leaking from some tank or something? Have you ever been inside the wreck?"

"Not in the bottom of the wreck. Before the ship was sunk, large holes were cut in the sides so divers could penetrate the hull, but only the upper decks. Lower decks are off-limits for safety reasons. Too many dark passageways where a diver could get hung up, entangled, or disoriented."

"Well, I think that I should go diving with you next time you go back there."

"I didn't know that you were a diver, Joe."

"Well, ah, actually I'm not. I mean, I'm a good swimmer. I've snorkeled before. I used to love going to the beach with my kids, riding waves and stuff like that. But I've never tried scuba. Listen, you're an instructor; how long would it take you to teach me what I need to know in order for me to be able to dive with you so we could investigate together?"

"Look, in one day I could teach you enough so you would be able to dive and not kill yourself, but you wouldn't be much of a help to me with that little training." Joe looked hurt by Terry's assessment of his ability to help in a meaningful way. "Hey, I didn't mean to sting your male pride, it's just that instead of doing any serious investigating, I'd have to keep my eye on you to make sure you didn't get into trouble down there."

"I think I could take care of myself," Joe said defensively.

"Joe, you can't believe how fast a novice or untrained diver can get into difficulty. If you don't know how to handle a problem, even a minor problem, panic sets in and then it's a downward spiral into a real dangerous situation. All I'm saying is that for what you want to accomplish, one day's training in a pool won't do it. You need a basic certification course, but I know I could compress the course into a few days, a week or so, and you'd do fine." Joe's mood brightened up upon hearing Terry's confidence in him.

"OK, let's start tonight!"

"Just what I like, an eager student," Terry laughed, "Hey, food's here!"

Chapter 27

Oscar maneuvered his boat into the shallows, waiting for his men to arrive with the cocaine. *Where the hell are those idiots?* he wondered, anxiously looking at his watch. *It's 10 o'clock and no sign of them!* Finally, he heard the sound of a truck in the distance, and soon he saw movement along the beach. He blinked a lantern twice and received two confirmation blinks in return. He moved in closer to the deserted beach.

"This is as far as I can go," he shouted, "Put the boxes on the rafts and swim out." The men did as they were told, and by 10:15 they began their slow ride out to the wreck of the *Felipe Xicotencatl.* Oscar kept to a slow pace, about three knots, in order to minimize engine noise and to avoid creating a visible bow wake, which sometimes could glow due to natural bioluminescence as the boat disturbed microscopic organisms in the water.

After about an hour, they arrived at the mooring buoy, which was tied to the bow of the wreck. Oscar secured his boat to the buoy, as the other three men, now fully dressed in the scuba gear that Oscar had brought, quietly slipped into the water. The men descended along the mooring line, each carrying a dive light, which would not be turned on until they had descended at least twenty feet. One of the divers hooked a separate line to the wreck, about amidships, the other end of which was secured to the boat. The other men then stationed themselves along this line, about every twenty feet. Oscar attached each of the boxes to this line with a snap-hook and the men guided the boxes down the line to the deck of the wreck, a depth of about fifty feet, and the divers carried the boxes through the openings cut into the hull amidships.

Once inside, they swam to a stairway leading to the next deck down, toward the stern. One man stayed at the opening of the stairway and held a reel with a line, similar to that used by cave divers. The lead diver tied the line to his BC and descended the stairway, followed by the other diver. No matter how many twists and turns they made, it would be relatively simple to follow the line back to the top of the stairway. Two decks below, they deposited all ten boxes, a total of about 200 kilos of cocaine, into a large, open storage room and left quickly.

Even with dive lights and the safety line to lead them back, the men were not comfortable inside the bowels of a sunken ship at night without direct access to the surface. It was an unsettling feeling even for experienced wreck divers. They unfastened the line, which had been used to guide the boxes down to the wreck, and swam toward a light that Oscar had lowered to serve as an underwater beacon, since he had intentionally let the boat drift away from the mooring buoy, in the unlikely event any boat traffic happened to pass by. The divers surfaced and, after boarding the boat and leaving the area, there was no indication that anyone had ever been there.

Terry and Joe had returned to her apartment after dinner, and Terry got out some student materials and gave them to Joe. "Here you go. This will get you started. Everything that you will need to know in order to pass the written part of the course is in here."

"Written part! You mean I have to pass a test?" Joe said, incredulous.

"Look, the idea here isn't for me just to teach you how to dive without killing yourself! It's also to get you a "C" card – a certification card – so you can dive anywhere in the world, using the card as evidence that you know what you are doing," Terry said in her best teacher's voice, as if she were trying to control an unruly class. "I can't authorize the issuance of a card to you by NAUI, my certifying organization, until you pass the written test and demonstrate proficiency in your open water skills."

"What if I don't pass the test?" Terry stepped toward Joe and narrowed her eyes. Putting her arms around him, she said, "Then I may have to keep you a prisoner here, until you do pass the test."

"Promise?"

"A promise is a promise!"

Class was over for the night.

Chapter 28

The next morning, Terry started Joe's training in earnest. After an overview of scuba equipment, explaining how BCs, regulators and tanks function and how to set up, break down and maintain the equipment, she took a short break to take care of her other business. Due to her time in the hospital and subsequent required abstinence from diving, she had to refer her customers to other dive operators. She was well known among the diving community on Cozumel, so she had a good network of friends to whom she could confidently refer business. Many of these same operators had referred customers to Terry when she was trying to get her own dive operation off the ground, so she was also happy to finally be able to reciprocate.

After the break, Terry resumed. "OK, now we'll cover what happens to the body underwater due to the effects of pressure, and diving problems caused by air expansion in the body, such as lung overpressure, which can result in a collapsed lung, called a pneumothorax, air embolism and a host of other medical dangers that can happen to a diver." When Terry suggested they break for lunch, Joe was only too happy to oblige. He wasn't sure if he was in dive class or had made a wrong turn and wound up in medical school by mistake.

He said to Terry, "I never realized there was so much to learn. I thought you just strapped on a set of tanks and off you went." Terry smiled, hearing Joe echo the same comment that she had made to Mark when she had begun her own dive lessons, so long ago.

"Well, it seems like a lot to learn, but after a while it'll seem like second nature. When we get in the water this afternoon, the pieces will start falling into place."

"Are we going to a reef today?"

"Not so fast, sailor. Pool lessons are first. You have some new skills to learn and the best place to do that is in the controlled environment of a pool."

After lunch, Terry loaded up her truck, drove to a tank-filling station to pick up a couple of tanks and headed off with Joe to a small hotel that had a pool where she usually took new students. She was friends with the owner, who let her use his facility for a small fee. At poolside, she taught Joe how to set up and put on the equipment, then it was into the pool to get comfortable with breathing underwater.

As she began teaching him the emergency skills of underwater mask clearing, regulator retrieval and others, the memory of Mark teaching her the same skills many years earlier flashed briefly through her mind, and she realized her life had come full circle. She felt he would be proud of her if he knew. *No*, she thought, *I'm sure he does know!*

As Terry drove Joe back to her apartment, his head was spinning from trying to absorb so much information in one day, especially because he knew that Terry would quiz him tonight on all he had learned today. "You did real well for the first day; how did you like it?

"Great." Joe said, enthusiastically. He was genuinely appreciative of his teacher's praise. When they arrived, Terry said, "Let's eat in tonight. I make great fajitas. Do you like chicken or beef?"

"Beef."

"I thought so; you look like a 'beefy' kind of guy. Let's shower off the chlorine first." After a quick shower together, Terry said, "Why don't you fix us some drinks while I start cooking."

"OK, margaritas?"

"No. I feel like a gin and tonic tonight."

"Sounds good. I'll join you." The quiz started while Joe was preparing the drinks and Terry was stir-frying some vegetables for the fajitas.

"What's the name of the clearing method where you pinch your nose and blow air gently through your Eustachian tubes to equalize pressure in the middle ear area behind your eardrum?" Joe's mind raced as he thought, *don't screw up now, Joe, old boy!*

"Valsalva maneuver!"

"Good. What do you do when you are descending and you can't go farther because of ear pain?"

"Go up a couple of feet to where you were last able to clear and then try again."

"Good. I'm impressed. Now what do you do when you start to ascend and you can't stop for your safety stop because the air you put into your BC at fifty feet has expanded so much at twenty feet that it is lifting you up too fast?"

Joe blinked. *Oh shit, what's the answer?* He couldn't recall; he drew a complete blank. He felt crushed, stupid, and inadequate. He had let Terry down; what would she think of him?

"Ah, sorry, I just don't recall." Joe thought, *she probably thinks I'm a dunce.*

"I know why you can't recall."

"Why?"

"That's getting into buoyancy control, which I didn't teach to you yet," Terry laughed.

"Why, you... you... "

"Devil?" Terry winked at him, coyly.

"Exactly!" Joe rushed her in a mock attack and they fell to the floor laughing. Terry rolled on top of Joe, pinning his arms to the floor. Her arms were very strong; lifting scuba tanks day in and day out will do that. As her long auburn hair fell into his eyes, she looked down at him very sternly and, as she lowered her lips to meet his, said in her most threatening voice, "It is not good for the students to attack their teacher that way!"

Dinner was severely burned that night.

Chapter 29

Earlier that same afternoon, at approximately 1 o'clock, the *Sea Queen* had arrived in Cozumel from Nassau, docking downtown. The local merchants looked forward to two days of good business as about 1,200 passengers spilled out onto the streets, seeking bargains and souvenirs of all kinds. Some tourists from the boat took taxicabs or mini buses for a fifteen minute ride to Chankanaab National Park for a day at the beach, featuring some of the best snorkeling in the Caribbean.

Later that night, at about 10 o'clock, while Terry and Joe were trying to salvage their burned fajitas, a group of five men assembled at one of the lower-deck exit locations on the *Sea Queen* and departed in one of the ship's motor launches. They were fully equipped with scuba equipment and, also, lift bags, which are inflated underwater and then used to lift heavy objects from the sea floor. In about thirty minutes they arrived at the mooring buoy of the wreck, *Felipe Xicotencatl*.

Four divers slipped into the water and swam to the mooring line, following it down to the bow of the wreck. They made their way to the openings in the side of the hull and then continued to retrace the route that Oscar's team had taken to get down to the storage room where the drug shipment was stored. The divers had made this trip several times before, and were able to work quickly and efficiently, even though the only light they had was supplied by the narrow beams of their dive lights.

They attached a lift bag to each box, inflating the bags with air from their regulators until the positive buoyancy of each bag made each box weightless. They removed all ten boxes, never noticing an eleventh box, part of an earlier shipment, which lay shattered in the corner of the room, with its contents of cocaine-laced, imitation coral having spilled out onto the floor of the storage area, and some in the sand outside the ship through a small hole in the hull. The team loaded the boxes onto the motor launch and returned to the *Sea Queen* with their booty, loading it aboard with the assistance of their accomplices on the ship.

The boxes were quickly put into storage and the ship's inventory records falsified to indicate that the boxes had been originally loaded in Miami; hence they would avoid being examined by U.S. Customs when the ship returned to the United States. Later that night, a coded radio message from the *Sea Queen* was received in Miami and the next day Oscar dialed his bank in the Cayman Islands to confirm that the correct amount of U.S. dollars had been deposited into his account.

Chapter 30

Terry and Joe ate breakfast as the odor of burned fajitas still hung in the air. "Boy, the smell of those burned onions really hangs in the air," Joe said.

"Well, that's what happens when students misbehave and distract the chef. OK, as soon as you finish your coffee, class is in session." Class lasted until early afternoon, and, as Joe was zoning out trying to use dive tables to calculate required surface interval times between dives, Terry said, "OK, let's head for the beach."

"No more pool stuff?"

"Nope; I've decided that you've advanced to the next level. We'll practice the same skills you learned yesterday, plus we'll go over buoyancy control." Now that Joe was developing familiarity with the subject matter, his learning pace accelerated. He breezed through a review of the skills he learned in the pool and quickly got the hang of controlling and adjusting his buoyancy under water.

That evening after dinner, Terry gave Joe another class lesson and then told him he would take his written test tomorrow, "After I help you relieve some stress and tension tonight."

Joe had learned not to argue with the teacher.

Oscar was also having dinner, but it was with his contact from the police station. "Well, Sergeant, anything else new about the report? Has the American bitch brought in any more dead fish?"

"No, senor Oscar," his contact respectfully said. "I haven't seen the American detective around, either."

"Good." Oscar was digesting this information carefully, because he had a big decision to make. He was thinking over the various options. *Do I look for a new drop site and abandon the most convenient, safest, best-concealed location anyone ever had for such an operation?* Oscar had used the wreck of the *Felipe Xicotencatl* as a drop site ever since the late Ricky had stumbled onto the idea while conducting a dive there as a dive master a year ago. *Too bad I had to kill him,* mused Oscar, *but, business comes first, and he became a danger to my business, a major liability.* It was the perfect set-up to complete a transaction that could not be conducted face-to-face.

The drugs were well hidden, in a location too dangerous for recreational divers to venture in daytime. The only divers who would even think of penetrating that deep inside a wreck were experienced wreck divers, and the *Felipe Xicotencatl* was not sufficiently challenging to attract such technically advanced divers. Furthermore, no one conducted night dives on a wreck, especially where the currents were usually at least moderately strong. Even if they did, they would never penetrate the wreck at night. No, it was the perfect site.

Oscar had the instincts of a gambler and succeeded by intuitively calculating the odds of success of his ventures. From the information that he had been told, it was premature to abandon this location. He decided that would continue to use it. "All right, just keep me informed of any sudden developments." He passed an envelope, thick with U.S. currency, to his contact, rose from his chair, turned around and left.

Chapter 31

Joe passed his written exam the next morning, getting only two answers, concerning the use of decompression dive tables, wrong.

"Hey, don't sweat the details," said Terry. "Almost everyone stumbles on those. The main thing is that you understand the concepts behind them and that you can use them to calculate your required surface intervals and depth limitations for a couple of repetitive dives. I don't think you will have to worry about more than two repetitive dives for a long time. Besides, that's when dive computers come in handy."

"What's on the agenda for today?"

"Your first boat dive, and then after a surface interval I thought you would like to see the wreck of the *Felipe Xicotencatl*, at least from the outside. Is that all right?"

"Would I!" Joe exclaimed. "This is what I've been *waiting*, no, make that *training*, for."

"And you've been a star pupil, too," said Terry, "one of the fastest learners I have ever had. You just need to complete your open-water dives today and tomorrow to certify. If you do a good job on your open-water dives today, I may even give you an early graduation present tonight."

"Now that's what I call an incentive," said Joe, grinning, "If I had teachers like you I would have graduated college with honors." As Joe moved closer to kiss Terry, she quickly sidestepped him and shoved him out the door.

"Get going, buddy. If I had you in college you would have been spent plenty of time in the dean's office."

They drove to the marina, where Manuel was already waiting with the boat. "Joe, help me with those tanks, please. We'll take five; two for each dive and one for a spare." They loaded the tanks and the rest of the dive gear and untied the fore and aft lines as Manuel skillfully backed away from the dock and headed the *Dorado* out into the channel.

"Chankanaab Reef, please, Manuel."

"We'll stay pretty much in one place today," she explained to Joe, "It's a good shallow dive for your first open-water boat dive, with lots of good stuff to see. Then after a surface interval we won't be far from the wreck."

"Sounds like a plan."

They reached the reef after a short ride and back-rolled into the water. Once they bobbed to the surface, Terry said, "You OK?"

Joe nodded affirmatively.

"We'll go down to about twenty feet and practice some skills, then just have some fun. Let's go!" As they descended, Joe had some difficulty equalizing his ears, but performed his equalizing techniques as he had been trained to do and continued down. At twenty feet, Terry held out her hand, palm down, to indicate, *Stop.*

As they hovered, Terry pointed to Joe, then to her own eyes, diver sign language for, *You watch me.* She then pulled her mask from her face, flooding it, then pressed the top skirt of the mask against her forehead and cleared it by exhaling through her nose. She then extended her hand toward Joe, palm up, sign language for, *Now it's your turn.* He did as he was instructed and then they went through all the other basic skills the same way.

After he had demonstrated proficiency in the required skills, Terry moved her hands in a clapping motion, her own sign language for, *Congratulations.* Joe smiled and, as he did, accidentally let some seawater into his mouth, which he blew out through his regulator. Terry noticed the puff of bubbles and realized what happened but just noted to herself, *Good, he didn't panic*. She then made a circle-sign with her thumb and forefinger and other three fingers extended, the "OK" sign. When Joe acknowledged, "OK," Terry pointed her thumb down to indicate, *Let's go deeper*. They reached the bottom at 40 feet and proceeded to move along with the slight current. Joe was amazed at the sea life he saw and tried to absorb everything while still being conscientious about monitoring his gauges.

After the dive, Manuel pointed the *Dorado* to a sheltered area of calm water where they could relax and eat a light snack. "So how did you like it?" Terry asked.

"WOW, that was great! Unbelievable! Was that a moray eel poking his head out from under that piece of rock?"

"Yep, a green moray. Looks a lot more fierce than he really is."

"How about that large stingray gliding along the bottom with that other large fish following him?"

"That was a southern stingray, hunting, being shadowed by a bar jack looking for scraps of food left by the stingray."

"Those colors of the sponges and corals were..." Terry smiled to herself, thinking of little Tommy Olsen, and cut Joe off in mid-exclamation.

"Awesome?"

"Yeah, pretty awesome. You get paid for doing this? Sign me up, I'll work for free!" Terry laughed and thought, *if I had had a dollar for every tourist who said that I could retire rich right now.*

"Well, it's not as glamorous as it seems, Joe. There's a lot of behind-the-scenes work that goes on. How do you think I got these?" Terry said, flexing her toned biceps.

"I know; I didn't mean to minimize what you do, but when you're down there it's just like, like..."

"Another world?" Terry said, finishing his thought again.

"Yeah, another world, kind of mystical, I don't know how to describe it."

"Well, just enjoy it. Besides, I couldn't hire you, anyway, you're not even certified yet," she laughed.

"Touché."

Joe had realized that he was deeply in love with Terry, even before today. Now, he felt not only his love growing for this amazing woman, but also his admiration and respect. She was not only incredibly attractive and sensual, but also intelligent, self-assured, adventurous and extremely capable. Joe wondered, *is there anything she can't do?* Having finally experienced, even in a limited way as a novice diver, what Terry did for a living, increased Joe's curiosity about her past, ten-fold.

"Terry, you never told me how you got into this business, how you got into scuba diving. It must be quite a story." Terry bit her lip as she looked away, avoiding Joe's eyes. She thought to herself, *oh you're right about that, Joe, it's quite a story.* She turned toward Joe and he noticed that her lips were pursed and her brow furrowed, as if she were fighting some internal battle.

"Well, I learned to scuba dive in Santa Barbara, California, where I lived at the time, about seven years ago. Then, when I moved to Monterey Bay California, I got my instructor's certification and taught diving there for a few years before coming here a couple of years ago. The rest of the stuff, about coming to Cozumel and working for Oscar, I told you already."

Joe didn't say anything, just waited for more information, one of his interrogation techniques that usually worked. The, "pregnant pause," they called it. After a few seconds of uncomfortable silence, the suspect would usually blurt out some useful piece of information that he was concealing. He could tell that Terry was struggling with something very important to her, but this was not the time or place to probe deeper.

"Thanks, I was just curious." It seemed to Joe that Terry was on the verge of telling him more but was just not ready to let him into that part of her life. Something, or someone, was already there.

After another thirty minutes Terry checked her dive computer, which indicated that sufficient time had elapsed since the last dive, so it was safe to dive again. "OK, let's go diving. Manuel, head for the *Felipe Xicotencatl.*" Manuel revved up the *Dorado's* engines and steered toward the mooring buoy, barely visible in the distance.

They reached the site and Terry said, "This will be a little different for you, actually easier because you can descend hand-over-hand on a line. Not that you have to, but try it for the experience. You'll see the top of the wreck as soon as you look down. You aren't certified to go deeper than 40 feet yet, so keep an eye on your depth gauge. When we get to 40 feet I'll assess how you're doing. If you feel comfortable at 40 feet give me the OK sign and if conditions are good I may decide to take you to 60 feet. Stay close as we go deeper and let me know if you want to stop or go back up. For a visual reference, don't go deeper than the top deck, and by all means don't go inside the ship on this dive." Joe simply nodded his acknowledgement. Terry was all business on a pre-dive briefing, and he enjoyed her take-charge, kick-ass attitude. *Wish I had a squad like her back in New York*, he thought. *We'd have the bad guys off the street in no time flat!*

As soon as Joe was beneath the surface he looked down and saw the wreck. It was only medium-sized as wrecks go, about 180 feet long with a thirty-five foot beam, but Joe had never seen anything like it underwater before and he was amazed to see something that big just sitting on the bottom of the sea. Terry wanted Joe to have fun and get used to swimming under water, so she dispensed with the skills practice.

Using hand signals, she asked Joe if he felt OK, pointing to Joe and making the OK sign. He responded affirmatively so they descended to the main deck, at about 60 feet, and slowly swam along the deck toward the stern. Terry noticed that the current was mild today but it still carried them past the stern. They reversed course and swam back against the current.

As they approached the stern, she saw Joe pointing to something just on the sea floor, below a small hole in the ship's hull. Terry saw that it was a piece of brain coral, and lying next to it was a piece of staghorn coral. Coral is usually named for what it looks like. Brain coral can be the shape and size of a basketball, a beach ball, or even larger. The polyps making up its surface are laid out in convoluted rows, looking surprisingly like a human brain. Staghorn coral looks like the spiky antlers of a deer. *Odd*, thought Terry, *you usually don't see these two types of coral in the same location.* Staghorn coral was usually seen in the shallower areas closer to shore, near the surf line, while brain coral is usually seen farther away from shore, in deeper water.

Joe knew that he was not supposed to descend past 60 feet, so he motioned to Terry to go down and bring it back. She wagged her finger, indicating "not allowed." Touching, and especially taking, any of the sea life in Cozumel was strictly prohibited by law. When he persisted, she slapped her hand against her wrist, to say, "no, you get punished." They looked at the coral for a few seconds, watching as several fish swam past, occasionally stopping to nibble at the coral, looking for algae or other tiny organisms that live in the coral.

Joe was amazed at the colors of the fish: multi-colored parrotfish, brilliant blue tangs, yellow tangs, and then a pair of strange-looking fish swimming side-by-side, flat-bodied with a long snout. He pointed them out to Terry and shrugged his shoulders, to say, *I don't know what those fish are.* Terry brushed her fingers across her nails, but Joe didn't get it. She would make a mental note to tell him later that they were filefish.

They did not see any dead fish, but as they continued to look, Joe pointed out a large, grey angelfish, swimming on its side. The current had moved them back away from the stern again and Terry wanted to conclude the dive soon, so she motioned for Joe to follow her and they swam toward the bow so they could use the mooring line as an ascent line when they were ready to surface.

They passed the coral once more, now being nibbled on by a small, colorful, yellow-and-black fish, called a rock beauty. As they passed the middle of the ship they looked down and saw a parrotfish swimming upside down in a jerky fashion, almost as if it were having convulsions. Something suddenly clicked in Terry's brain and she stopped so quickly that Joe shot right passed her. He turned to see her swimming toward the bottom and pick up both the brain and the staghorn coral.

He shrugged his shoulders to ask her, "What's going on?" but she gave him the thumbs-up sign to say, "Go up to the surface, now." They swam the ascent line and surfaced after their safety stop.

"What's up? I thought you said we couldn't take any coral?"

"Look, we were watching these fish nibble on the coral and then we see sick fish in the immediate vicinity. Don't you think there could be a connection?"

"I don't know. Do fish get sick from eating coral?"

"Well, fish don't eat coral per se. They are usually looking for algae and other little animals, which live in the coral for protection and nourishment. But in doing so, they may ingest some of the coral and excrete it later as sand, usually with no ill effects."

"Can coral get contaminated?'

"I don't know, but this stuff looks strange. It isn't living coral, it looks more like the dead skeleton of a coral that you see in souvenir shops or what they sell in some pet store for fish tanks." Terry sniffed it. "It smells funny, too. I think we should bring this to my friend, Doctor Sanchez, and let him analyze it. Manuel, let's head home. By the way, Joe, you did great on your dives today. After tomorrow's dives I can send your certification papers into NAUI."

"Thanks, 'teach,' you were a pretty good instructor."

When they arrived back at the marina it was too late to bring the coral to Doctor Sanchez for analysis, so they returned to Terry's apartment to take showers. "I'm not in the mood to cook tonight," she said. "Let's go to Pancho's."

"Fine by me. Let's go. I'm hungry."

"That was a southern stingray, hunting, being shadowed by a bar jack looking for scraps of food left by the stingray."

Photo by Paul J. Mila

As soon as Joe was beneath the surface he looked down and saw the wreck.....Joe had never seen anything like it underwater, and he was amazed to see something that big just sitting on the bottom of the sea

Photo by Paul J. Mila

Chapter 32

When Terry and Joe walked into Pancho's, the waiter remembered them and began to take them to a secluded corner table, when someone yelled out. "Hola, Senorita Terry!" Terry turned toward the speaker and saw it was her friend, Hector Suarez, with whom she had shared an apartment when she arrived in Cozumel. He was with a group of his friends, including Raul Pagan, who had sent her to see Oscar at Playa Divers for her first job. She was delighted to see him. After all, she thought, it wasn't Raul's fault that Oscar was a pig, and probably worse.

"Won't you and your friend join us?" Hector asked. Terry jumped at the opportunity, partly to see old friends that she had not seen in many months, but more so because she feared that in a secluded setting Joe would resume his questions into her past, a past that she was not yet ready to share.

"How wonderful to see you all! This is my good friend Joe Manetta."

"Hey, any friend of Senorita Terry is a friend of ours! Sit down and join us."

"Nice to meet you, too," said Joe, doing his best to seem enthusiastic. *Oh well*, he thought, *when in Rome...*

After dinner, Joe wasn't sure if Terry was just going to take him back to his hotel or to her apartment. She had been acting somewhat strangely at dinner, a little distant. Then again, earlier today she had promised him an early graduation present. Terry drove straight to her apartment. They sat in the kitchen and Terry said, "How about a night cap?"

"Sounds great, what do you have?"

"Amaretto, brandy, tequila, whatever you like."

"Amaretto on the rocks, please."

"Sounds good. I think I'll have one, too." After she poured the drinks they clinked glasses. "Good diving today, Joe, you did great. Tomorrow on the way to the marina I want to drop off that coral with Doctor Sanchez and have him take a look at it. It's the strangest coral I have ever seen. Look how it just crumbles with a little pressure. Coral is harder than that."

"Maybe it was sick or something before it died," suggested Joe. "Listen, Terry, I have to ask you something." The detective side of Joe's nature was kicking in. He saw Terry's features harden and he noticed every muscle in her body tense. "This afternoon when I asked you about how you learned to dive and how you got into teaching scuba, you just gave me a chronological record of your past. That's not what I was asking," *time for a little interrogative pressure.* "And I think you know it! Scuba diving isn't on everyone's list of top things to do. Something or someone triggered a passion in you to do it. I realized that today on my first boat dive. I never had any interest in learning to scuba dive before. Even when I asked you to teach me, I just did it initially because I thought it would help my investigation."

Joe sensed Terry's resolve to keep her past a secret beginning to waver. This was what he had been trained for, to go for the jugular when his subject weakened, but he couldn't do it to Terry; he eased up. "But one dive into your world gave me a whole different perspective on so many things, including you. I've never met anyone like you before and, well, I'm in love with you, Terry – very much."

174

Terry felt her heart skip a beat. She was torn by conflicting emotions and she tried to lighten the mood with a joke. "You mean like when patients fall in love with their nurse?" Joe would not be deflected; the detective in him resumed control.

"You know exactly what I mean, Terry, and I think you feel something for me, too!" Terry knew only too well that Joe was correct. She knew that she was in love with him. "And you also know what I'm really asking about." Terry knew that also, which scared her even more than letting Joe know her feelings about him.

"Yes Joe, you're right. I'm in love with you, too. Oh God, I never thought I would ever hear myself say that to anyone else again!" Terry covered her face with her hands for a moment and thought, *OK. If I love this man, I cannot keep secrets. It's time.* Joe watched her carefully, not knowing what he was going to hear as Terry began.

"Almost eight years ago while I was in college, I met Mark Stafford." Hearing herself say Mark's name out loud made Terry pause and she clasped the gold diver on the chain around her neck for strength. *Get a hold of yourself!* "He taught me how to dive; he taught me so many things." Terry went on to tell Joe everything about her relationship with Mark, about how close they had become to getting engaged, and about his violent death.

When she had finished, neither spoke a word for about a minute. Finally, Joe got up from his chair, walked over to Terry and knelt next to her. He put his arms around her and pulled her to him and kissed her gently. "Terry, I do love you."

"I love you, too, Joe, very much." There wasn't anything else to say. The got up and went into the bedroom, but they did not make love this night. The emotional intensity of the evening had left them both drained. They went to sleep in each other's arms, holding each other tightly, as if they were afraid that the other wouldn't be there in the morning.

It had also been a busy night for Oscar and his men. They had just dropped another shipment of cocaine in the storage room of the *Felipe Xicotencatl,* in preparation for a visit tomorrow from another cruise ship, the *Caribbean Queen,* coming in from Jamaica before continuing on to Miami.

Chapter 33

The next morning on their way to the marina, Terry and Joe stopped at the hospital to show Doctor Sanchez what they had found and asked him to analyze it. "Strange, it doesn't look or feel like real coral to me, either," he said, examining the "coral." He took the staghorn coral and snapped off a six-inch length. "Look at this; real coral doesn't break like this. See this powder residue where I broke it?"

"Can I have that piece?" asked Joe.

"Sure, here." Doctor Sanchez gave the piece that he had broken off to Joe, who put it in his pocket.

"We have some diving to do, Eduardo. When do you think you will know what this stuff is?" asked Terry.

"Call me first thing tomorrow morning. I should have some answers for you."

"Thanks very much, Eduardo. Talk to you tomorrow," said Terry, kissing him affectionately on the check as they left.

"I need to make one more stop before we go to the pier," said Joe, "to the police station."

"OK, it's on the way."

"Wait here, I'll just be a minute," said Joe as Terry parked in front of the station. Joe walked into the police station and went directly into sergeant Gonzalez' office. "Hola, Rafael, how are you today?"

"Fine, Joe, what can I do for you?"

"See this piece of what looks like coral? I need this to be sent via a special courier to my headquarters in New York, to this person's attention." Joe said as he wrote down the name of 'Bill Ryan' on an envelope and enclosed a short note with instructions.

"No problem," said Rafael Gonzalez. "We can arrange to get it there in a special diplomatic pouch by tomorrow."

"Thanks, Rafael. This may be the break we've been looking for. I'm running late now, so I'll call you later to explain."

When Terry and Joe got to the marina, Manuel was already there. Terry said, "Sorry we're late, Manuel. Let's get our stuff aboard and shove off." In about 20 minutes they were at the dive site. "Well, Joe, you need two more open-water dives. I figured we would combine some more investigating with your certification dives."

"Sounds good to me. What's the plan?"

"Technically, you're not supposed to go deeper than sixty feet, but I know you can handle eighty feet. There isn't that much difference, as long as there are no problems with the visibility and current. So, let's do a more thorough search around the wreck. Are you OK with that?"

"Sure, let's do it!"

Manuel moored the *Dorado* to the buoy marking the location of the wreck and Terry and Joe rolled into the water and began their descent. They went to the stern section, where they had seen the coral and sick fish yesterday. As they made their way along the sea floor at eighty-five feet, they saw more fish swimming strangely, in circles and upside down, entering and leaving through a small hole that led into the hull. There was no more coral outside the ship.

They made their way up to the large openings cut into the hull just below the main deck. Here they saw two dead angelfish and more sick fish near a stairway leading down to a lower deck, off-limits to divers. They had been under for about thirty minutes when Terry signaled Joe to begin their ascent.

Back on the boat Joe asked, "Why such a short dive?"

"I didn't want to accumulate too much nitrogen in my body because I want to do another dive again soon, maybe a little longer and a little deeper. Whatever is causing the problem is somewhere inside that ship, probably in a lower deck. Next dive I'm going inside to take a look."

"By yourself?"

"Well, wreck penetration is something you're definitely not trained to do."

"No way you're going in alone," protested Joe. Terry could see he would not be deterred and thought for a minute.

"OK, I have an idea." Joe watched as she opened a locker under the seats that were along the side of the boat. She took out four underwater dive lights, a cave reel, similar to the one used by Oscar's men, and another line of rope, about fifteen feet long. "We each take two dive lights, the larger one is your main, and the smaller one is a spare. If the main one goes out for any reason we use the spare and abort the dive. Understood?" Joe nodded affirmatively. "We tie the end of the rope from the cave reel to the ladder where we go down the stairwell and play out the reel as we go. On the way back, we follow the line to get out. Now, we tie one end of this other rope to each other, like a tether, so we can't get separated. You will follow me. If you get snagged on something, feel claustrophobic, have any problem at all, tug on the rope to get my attention and we are outta there. Agreed?"

"OK, boss."

"Any questions? Are we clear?"

"Like crystal," said Joe. During the forty-five minute surface interval, Joe was extremely quiet, as he pondered what it would be like to penetrate the inside of the wreck for the first time. His inner voice taunted him. *Well, Joe, ol' boy, let's hope you haven't finally bitten off more than you can chew!* Terry noticed his unusual demeanor and recognized it for what it was: the anxiety of a diver about to encounter an unfamiliar situation. Terry hoped it would not progress past normal mild anxiety into a full-blown panic attack. Finally, she said, "OK, let's do it. Any problems, we err on the side of caution."

"Got it!" Joe said, trying to sound more confident than he felt.

They rolled backward into the water and retraced their route, back to the stairway under the main deck. Terry expertly tied one end of the cave reel rope to the ladder of the stairwell, turned on her light as Joe did the same, and entered the dark passageway, with Joe tethered to her, following about fifteen feet behind.

Descending the narrow passageway with the darkness broken only by the narrow beams of their dive lights, Joe had to fight down a feeling of claustrophobia and panic. *She was right, this doesn't feel good. Get me out of here! No, control yourself, you're ok, just go slow, breathe slower.*

After a few turns through more passageways, they dropped through a hatch and were inside a large storage room. Joe was totally disoriented and made sure that he had a firm hold on the rope line that led back out to safety. They played their lights around the perimeter of the room and saw numerous dead and decaying fish, and then saw several boxes stacked against one of the bulkheads. They noticed a small shaft of natural light penetrating the darkness and saw the hole in the hull that they had seen when they were outside earlier.

They pointed their lights toward the hole, and next to it saw another box, identical to the ones that were stacked across the room, except that this box had fallen against a jagged piece of metal and had been ripped open. The contents, pieces of "coral," were strewn across the floor, being nibbled on by fish. Terry made her way to the stack of boxes on the other side of the room and, removing her dive knife from its sheath strapped to her calf, ripped through the top box, revealing more "coral." She removed several samples from the box, placing them into a small mesh bag that she carried, and then motioned to Joe to lead the way to the exit by following the rope line. Joe was happy to oblige.

Back on board they were excited and animated. "That was the mother lode," Terry said. "Did you see all that stuff? Look at this," she said, showing Joe the sample that she retrieved, "This is the same type of stuff that we found outside the ship yesterday!" Joe was hyperventilating, trying to catch his breath. "Hey, are you OK?"

"Yeah, just a little shaky from being down there inside that dark space, knowing I just couldn't get right up to the surface if I had to."

"That's OK. It's a confidence thing. You did great, especially given that you had no training for wreck penetration and you really shouldn't have been in there in the first place."

"Thanks; if you hadn't warned me ahead of time about what it would feel like, I think I would have bolted."

"And left me all alone? Thanks a lot! What a dive buddy you turned out to be!"

"Sorry, partner," said Joe as they shared a well-earned laugh.

"Anyway, you passed with flying colors. Let's head in. I think I owe you a graduation present."

As they drove away from the marina, Joe said, "That opened box looked like it had been there for some time, but the others looked like they had been placed there pretty recently."

"Yes, I was thinking the same thing. Why do you think they were left there?"

"Well I could be wrong, but I think they are waiting to be picked up, very soon." They drove the rest of the way in silence, speculating on the ramifications of what they had uncovered.

They showered back at Terry's apartment, and as Joe was getting dressed in the bedroom he heard a loud "pop" in the kitchen. He turned around to see Terry standing in the doorway, dressed only in a short, terry cloth robe, holding a chilled bottle of champagne in one hand and two glasses in the other. "Graduation time," she said seductively.

Chapter 34

At nine o'clock the next morning, the phone rang and Terry reached for it. "Hello," she said in a sleepy voice.

"Terry, it's Eduardo; I have some very important news!" Terry was jolted into alertness.

"Yes?"

"The 'coral' that you and detective Manetta found was not coral but almost one-hundred percent cocaine!"

"Cocaine?!"

"Yes. I said 'almost' because there was another substance mixed in, maybe five or ten percent of the volume, but I don't have the proper equipment to determine what it is. Perhaps it is some kind of binding material, which enabled them to cast the cocaine into the shape of coral."

"Joe, it's cocaine!" Joe had been half-listening, in a champagne-induced hangover.

"Is detective Manetta there with you now?" *Oops*, thought Terry, visualizing the Doctor's raised eyebrows, *I really spilled the beans this time.*

"Ah, yes, yes he is," said Terry trying to regain her composure. "Let me put him on."

"Hello Doctor, it sounds like you have interesting news."

"Ah, yes," said Doctor Sanchez, trying not to sound judgmental about where Joe had spent the night. "As you probably heard me telling Miss Hunter, the supposed coral is composed of about ninety percent cocaine and about ten percent of some other substance. I was just going to inform Sergeant Gonzalez."

"Doctor, would you mind holding off until I have had a chance to talk to him? I have my reasons. After we have spoken you can give him your full report."

"Well, this is most irregular, but yes, I will wait."

"Thank you, I'll explain later. Thanks again for your cooperation."

"What's up, Joe?" Terry asked after he hung up.

"I have some concerns about how information is handled at that police station."

"You mean like leaks? Do you suspect there is an informer?"

"Well, it just seems that your buddy Oscar is always a step ahead of us. You know, not being around when we went to question him, these 'accidents' that befall dive masters, things like that. Where drugs are involved there's a lot of money and where there's a lot of money there's corruption, usually aimed at politicians and the police. Let's get dressed and get over to see the good sergeant."

As they were getting ready to leave, the phone rang again. Terry handed the phone to Joe, saying, "Joe, it's for you – someone named Bill Ryan."

"Hello, Bill, what's up?"

"Well, I left a message at your hotel and then I called the secondary number that you wrote in the note that you sent with your little package. Who is that who answered the phone with the sweet voice?" Ryan asked, sarcastically.

"Oh, just someone who is helping me with the investigation."

"Really? Does she look as half as good in person as she sounds on the phone?"

"What's up, Bill?" Joe asked sharply. Bill Ryan was amused by the defensive tone in his partner's voice.

"Well, Joe-boy, you hit the jackpot." Terry saw Joe's eyes widen. "Your friend Sarah tested it for us and guess what? Not only was that little sample you sent composed of cocaine, but it also contained the glue marker, in exactly the same concentration that we saw in the stuff we found up here. In short, it's identical, the same stuff. Where'd you get it?" Terry jumped as Joe slammed his hand on the table.

"God damn, how about that!" he exclaimed. He told Bill the whole story.

"OK," said Bill, I'll inform the task force and we'll call you at the police station in one hour. Good job, buddy."

Joe told Terry what Bill Ryan and the New York Lab had found out. He said, "We have no time to lose. Let's get to the police station." When they arrived, they were immediately brought into Sergeant Gonzalez's office. "Rafael, I think we cracked this case," Terry excitedly began, even before Rafael had a chance to welcome them to his office. Joe told him of the results of Doctor Sanchez's analysis and what the police lab in New York had determined. Rafael expressed surprise that the doctor had not also called him with his information.

"Well, I'm afraid that's my fault, Rafael. I asked him to wait until I had spoken to you because I suspect that there may be a leak in your office, someone informing Oscar of every development."

"That would explain some of the events that have transpired," Rafael agreed.

"Well, I have some suggestions for you on how to handle that, but first let's try to figure out how the cocaine is being transferred. We already know they are using cruise ships to bring the drugs into the U.S., through Miami. It looks to me like Oscar is using the *Felipe Xicotencatl* as a transfer stop. They bring the cocaine there and hand it off to someone who will actually smuggle it out on a cruise ship. When is the next ship due to arrive?"

"Today," said Rafael, "The *Caribbean Queen* is coming in at eleven o'clock, about now. She was supposed to come in yesterday, but was delayed due to mechanical trouble."

"That means the boxes are probably still in the wreck," said Terry, "If the *Caribbean Queen* had been on schedule they would have been transferred aboard the liner last night. I don't think they would risk a daytime transfer, not with all the boat traffic in the area."

"So they will probably move the drugs tonight," said Joe. "Rafael, can you arrange resources for continual surveillance for the next 24 to 48 hours?"

"Yes, what else do you need?"

"A team of a couple of men on shore to keep the *Caribbean Queen* under observation until she leaves, and one team with a fast boat and several experienced divers to stake out the *Felipe Xicotencatl*. We could also use some night-vision observation equipment – you know, infrared scopes and that kind of stuff."

"I can obtain a patrol boat, the necessary men, and a couple of divers. I'm afraid we don't have any sophisticated nighttime equipment."

"Don't worry about it. I can make a phone call to task force headquarters in Miami and have whatever high-tech equipment we need flown here in four or five hours."

"Fine, I will meet with my staff and begin to assemble our team. Let's meet back here at six o'clock."

"OK, I'll go back to my hotel and start coordinating resources from our strike force in the U.S." As they left the building and walked to Joe's car, Terry said, "If you think Rafael is the leak, you sure gave him an awful lot of information about your plans."

"Well, it's a gamble, Terry. I need to let him think I still trust him so I can't start withholding information now or I'd tip him off that I suspect him. And if he is the leak, maybe the extra pressure on him will make him slip up. We'll just have to wait, be extra careful, and see how it plays out. I hope he's still one of us, though. I really like the guy."

Joe and Terry drove back to his hotel so he could contact the Miami task force, give them the latest update and request the equipment that they would need. Terry was unusually quiet on the way back, noticing the change in Joe. Up until now she had been pretty much in charge, teaching him how to dive, taking care of him. Now, in this phase of the operation, the police training in him was taking over and he was asserting himself. She had never really seen this side of him. She didn't know how she felt about giving up control, giving up the lead.

When they arrived, Joe immediately started setting up his satellite communication equipment and contacted the task force on a secure link. He gave his progress report and requested the night-vision equipment. "OK, roger that, Detective Manetta. Your package will arrive at Cozumel International Airport at 1700, local time."

Joe was so focused that he had not noticed that Terry had not said a word since leaving the police station. Finally, he said to her, "Hey, cat got your tongue? What's up? Can you believe we're really going to take them down?"

"What's my role? How can I help?"

"Beyond what you have already done? You started this whole chain of events. You found the sick and dead fish and had the foresight to have them analyzed, trained me to dive so I could help you investigate and you made all the connections."

"So what do I do now? Sit back and do nothing? I have a personal stake in this."

"Right. I forgot to add, you almost got yourself killed by these people. I think you've done enough as a private citizen."

"Don't patronize me, goddamn it! Are you telling me now to be a 'good little girl' and sit back while the 'pros' take over? No way!"

Joe was temporarily taken aback. He had never seen this side of Terry before. He knew she was tenacious, headstrong and passionate, but he had never experienced the fury of her temper before. Finally he regrouped, held her tightly by the shoulders and tried, as he saw it, to shake some sense into her.

"What I'm telling you is that you did a damn good job; if it wasn't for you I'd still be chasing my stupid t-shirt theory, here or on some other island; I'm telling you that I'm afraid that you might get hurt and I don't want to lose you; I'm telling you that, well, I don't know if it's God, or fate or whatever, but someone or something has given both of us a second chance at happiness and I don't want to throw it away!"

He tried to kiss her but she ran past him, crying, out of the apartment, jumped into her car and drove away, tires squealing. He knew that she was determined to make sure that she would be one of the divers on the patrol boat tonight.

Chapter 35

A few minutes after Sergeant Rafael Gonzalez had his staff meeting, a phone call was made from the police station to Oscar's office at Playa Divers. "I have the worst possible news for you, senor."

Oscar was in a rage, powerless to do anything about the situation. He couldn't retrieve the drugs during the daytime, not with recreational divers all over the wreck, which would probably be under surveillance, anyway. He couldn't contact the pickup team on the ship. He did not know who they were. For security purposes, neither the delivery team nor the pickup team knew the other's identity. All he could do was cut his losses and go into survival mode and start over somewhere else.

He opened a safe in his office and removed $200,000, his emergency fund, which he kept in the event he would have to quickly escape one day. As he packed up a few other things, he thought about how this had happened, how his profitable operation had been ruined, who had started his downfall. He would have to flee, but before that he would get revenge.

The strike force met in Rafael's office. One team was dispatched to the downtown dock area, where the *Caribbean Queen* was docked. The patrol boat with Joe, Rafael and a team of six divers, including Terry, headed out to an area far enough away from the wreck to avoid detection. The plan was for the on-shore surveillance team stationed at the dock to notify the patrol boat when the drug runners left the ship. Once the patrol boat saw the motor launch, they would move closer under cover of darkness, with no running lights on the boat.

When they were in range, one team of three divers would slip into the water with their own dive lights turned off and hover at thirty feet, a depth where they could easily stay for an hour, and watch for the underwater lights of the divers descending to the wreck. If they had to wait under water for over an hour they would surface and the second team would go in. They would alternate underwater surveillance until the pickup was made. Terry was in the second group of three divers.

At about 9 o'clock, the patrol boat got the signal from the shore team. A motor launch was leaving the *Caribbean Queen* and was on a heading toward the wreck. The patrol boat moved into position and, using the night-vision equipment supplied by the Miami task force, observed the motor launch from a distance. As the motor launch neared the mooring buoy at the wreck, the first three police divers slipped into the water and waited. Nothing happened. Were the smugglers waiting to see if they had been followed?

At the one-hour mark, Terry and the other divers of the second team slipped into the water and replaced the first team. After fifteen minutes, underwater lights appeared faintly in the distance as the pickup team entered the water and descended to the wreck. The police divers watched and waited patiently, until they saw the dive lights rising back toward the surface about a half-hour later; then they returned to the police boat.

"They're up, the drugs are on board!" said Terry as the dive team surfaced and quickly boarded. "OK, let's take them," ordered Rafael Gonzalez. The motors came to life as the patrol boat quickly raced in. The *Caribbean Queen's* motor launch tried to get away, but was no match for the speed of the police boat. A quick burst from a 50-caliber machine gun fired across the bow of the launch quickly brought it to a halt.

The police team aimed searchlights at the motor launch and, using loudspeakers, ordered the crew to freeze. They saw that the drug runners were trying to dump the cocaine overboard, but succeeded in throwing only several boxes into the water before they were boarded and subdued. Joe and Rafael had hoped to snare Oscar in their trap, but were disappointed that he was not aboard. Rafael radioed a third team that had been dispatched to Playa Divers to apprehend Oscar, but learned that he had evaded them, as well. He turned to Joe and said, "As you said, my friend, our elusive prey always seems to be one step ahead of us."

By eleven o'clock the operation was all over and the team was back at the police station with the prisoners and the cocaine. Joe immediately contacted task force headquarters to notify them of the success of the operation. There were congratulatory handshakes and backslaps all around, and Rafael broke out some expensive tequila to celebrate. Joe quickly bonded with his brother police officers and, with Rafael serving as translator to help mend Joe's broken Spanish, the evening consisted of exchanging and comparing stories about their police exploits.

After several rounds of toasts, Joe looked for Terry, but she had left. "Damn!' he said. In the post-adrenaline-rush of the successful operation he had totally forgotten about Terry and, feeling like an outsider, she was hurt. Joe knew he would have some patching up to do, but for now it was time to celebrate with the guys.

Chapter 36

Early the next morning, Police Officer Sergeant Juan Rivera, one of Sergeant Gonzalez's most trusted senior officers, was sitting at his desk when a call came in. "Officer Rivera here," he said. He immediately sat up at attention when he heard the voice on the other end of the line. "But senor, I cannot do that. I agreed only to give you information. I never..." Then the color drained from his face as he finally realized what it meant to be in league with the Devil. As he listened to a terrifying description what would happen to his wife and children if he did not obey, he simply said, "Yes, senor. I will do as you instruct."

When he hung up the phone his uniform was soaked with perspiration. He composed himself and dialed the number he had been given.

"Hello, Terry Hunter speaking. Oh hello, officer Rivera." The disappointment was obvious in her voice as she had hoped it would be Joe calling. "Yes, I can be there right away. OK, I'll be glad to help. See you there, goodbye."

She decided to call Joe, even though it was only 5:30 in the morning. No answer. Joe was still sleeping off the effects of too much tequila during his night of macho revelry with the members of the jubilant strike team.

Terry decided to leave a message. "Hi Joe, Terry here. It's about 5:30 and Officer Rivera just called me. They need a diver to help recover the rest of the cocaine that was dumped overboard last night, and no one else is available, so I'm meeting him at the marina. I guess I'll see you later. Maybe we can have lunch, if you can squeeze me in." The sarcastic edge in her tone was very apparent, deliberately so.

Terry hung up and left for the marina. The ringing of the phone woke Joe, but he was in a haze, and did not pick up the receiver until Terry had hung up. When he heard her message on voice mail he shook his head to clear the cobwebs and played the message again. It just didn't seem right. He called Terry back but got no answer. Then, he called Rafael at home and woke him up. "Rafael, are you planning to recover the rest of the cocaine that was dumped overboard last night?"

"Eventually, but there is no rush. We have plenty for evidence."

"That's what I thought." He then told Rafael about the strange call that he had just received from Terry.

"Oh my God!" said Rafael. "I was going to tell you today that I followed your suggestion to tap all of our outgoing lines at the station. It seems that several calls were made to Oscar's private office number at Playa Divers, and they were made from Officer Rivera's phone." A chill ran down Joe's spine.

"She's walking into a trap! We have to get to the marina fast, I'll meet you there."

When Terry got to the marina, Officer Rivera was already there on the boat. It was tied up so closely to the dock that Terry could not see the name painted on the bow, *Santa Rosa II,* the largest and fastest of the Playa Divers dive boats. She boarded and the captain at the helm eased the boat into the channel.

Several minutes later, Joe and Rafael pulled into the marina parking lot. Joe looked down the row of boats, still moored in their slips since it was too early for the boats to pick up their morning dive customers. He spotted Manuel sleeping on the deck of the *Dorado.*

Joe shook him out of a sound sleep. "Terry's in trouble, we have to get out there and help her. Manuel cleared his head, ran to the bridge of the *Dorado,* fired up the engines and, several minutes later, pulled out of the marina with Joe and Rafael.

"Which way?" Joe wasn't sure where the drugs had been dumped in the dark.

"Toward the wreck, quickly," Rafael ordered, figuring once they were in the vicinity they would spot the boat easily, since there would not be many other dive boats out on the water this early in the morning.

When the *Santa Rosa II* reached the vicinity of the Chankanaab Reef, the motors stopped. "Hey, this isn't where the drugs were dumped last night. We have to go farther out," said Terry.

"It's as far as you're going, bitch," came an ominously familiar voice from the door leading to the cabin below deck. Terry stared at the doorway incredulously, as the form of Oscar materialized in front of her. All she could see were his eyes. She saw the same cold, hateful look that she had seen several years ago, the day after he had tried unsuccessfully to rape her.

As Oscar stepped toward Terry, she stepped back toward the stern. Her mind was racing. *Do I jump overboard? No, I'll just become another boating accident.* She took one more step back and suddenly her arms were pinned as Officer Rivera grabbed her from behind. Oscar grinned and stepped forward.

Terry kicked out, but Oscar sidestepped and buried his fist in Terry's mid-section, knocking the wind out of her. Her head pitched forward and her knees buckled as Rivera held her up. She screamed in pain as Oscar grabbed her hair and pulled her head up so Terry could see him.

"You once said that you would kill me if I ever touched you again, eh?" Terry was still gasping for breath and never saw the right cross coming until Oscar's fist smashed flush against her left jaw and everything went black.

Terry woke up on her stomach and tried to move her arms, only to find that her wrists were tied behind her back. She tried to move her legs and discovered that her ankles were also tied together. As she tried to clear her head, she felt Oscar tying a weight belt around her waist. "Why don't we just shoot her and dump her overboard? Or we can run her over with the boat – it will seem like an accident," suggested Rivera. *You fool*, thought Oscar, *that's what I have planned for you, next.* As far as Oscar was concerned, Rivera was just another loose end that would have to be cleared up soon, another liability.

Oscar roared, "No! I want to watch her drown, slowly. I want to see her suffer, to beg me to save her; to see her face looking up at me from under water, to see her eyes imploring me to pull her out, until they go blank, in death."

Rivera is right, this is madness; we should just kill her fast and get out of here, thought Oscar's partner, piloting the *Santa Rosa II*. He was Oscar's most trusted associate in his gang, and Oscar had decided to flee Cozumel with him. Their plan was to take the boat to Cancun and then catch a private plane that Oscar already had hired to take them to Mexico City. From there, they could decide on a safe international location. But he had known Oscar for many years and knew that when he had something in mind, no matter how irrational or bizarre, it was useless to try to dissuade him. So, Oscar would have his revenge first.

Oscar rolled Terry over on her back and lifted her feet while Rivera lifted her under her arms. Together they swung her like a sack of potatoes. "OK, on three – one, two, three!" Over the side she went, into the water. Terry was wearing a wet suit and was buoyant enough to have easily floated, even tied as she was. But Oscar had attached six pounds of lead weight to her weight belt, just enough to make her negatively buoyant, though not enough to sink her fast.

As Terry went under, she was able to move her body in a undulating motion and kick with her feet tied together, in what is called a "dolphin" kick, as opposed to the usual "flutter" kick that swimmers and divers commonly use when they kick their feet separately. But, as Oscar had planned, as soon as Terry kicked her way to the surface, exhaled and gulped a lungful of fresh air, she would sink again. Eventually she would tire, become too tired to kick. She would hold her breath until her lungs burned, finally taking in a mouthful of water, triggering the gag reflex, then a cough, then she would gasp a lungful of water and drown. It would be slow and tortuous. And Oscar would enjoy every second of it.

Terry had been repeatedly sinking and kicking back to the surface for almost fifteen minutes. Her will to live was strong, but her body was starting to tire, her muscles losing the battle against oxygen starvation, starting to cramp. Her brain was in a battle with itself, part of it trying to rationalize and convince Terry's conscious mind that it should let go, to accept death, *then you can see Mark again;* part of it trying to convince her to fight death, fight to live, *you want a life with Joe, don't you?*

Rivera suddenly yelled out, "Shark! Coming toward the bow!" Oscar looked up and saw the triangular fin cutting through the water. He could not believe his good fortune. His warped mind thought, *if only the shark could get in a bite or two before she drowns she would die in pain; I would be so happy.*

He vaguely recalled some rumor he had heard when Terry worked at Playa Divers, about her boyfriend or lover being killed by a shark back in the States several years earlier. *Maybe this was the same shark?* He laughed at the improbable thought, as he glanced at the fin slicing purposefully through the water, coming closer. He looked down as Terry gulped another breath and sank again. Then, the fin disappeared under the surface as the fish closed on her. Terry felt a bump, and then the sensation of being lifted toward the surface.

Just as Oscar was gleefully looking for a telltale blood slick, he was horrified to see that it was not a shark, but a dolphin and it was supporting Terry on the surface, on its back. Rivera had never spent much time on the water and could not distinguish between the curved, sickle-shape of a dolphin's dorsal fin from the more pointed dorsal fin of a shark.

Oscar should have known better, but he was so focused on killing Terry that his eyes had tricked his mind into seeing what he wanted to see. Terry took a few deep breaths of air and looked back to see healed scars from a fishing net on the dolphin's skin. She realized it was Lucky, probably cruising through the area to visit his captive friends a couple of miles away at the Chankanaab Dolphin Encounter facility. The young dolphin had scanned Terry's body with his echolocation sonar and sensed that she was in distress.

Oscar saw that the dolphin was pushing Terry toward shore as it balanced her on its back and screamed, "No! I'll kill both of you!" He pulled out a knife and dove into the water, swimming after the dolphin and Terry. He caught up and plunged the knife into the side of the young dolphin. In pain, Lucky let out a series of high-pitched whistles and loud clicks, but would not leave Terry. Oscar pulled the knife out and plunged it again into the belly of the dolphin as Terry tried to kick him away, in vain.

Then, just as Oscar was about to kill Terry, the mother dolphin, Notchka, who had been swimming nearby and had seen her offspring attacked, put on a burst of speed, dipped down and then propelled herself upward, striking Oscar in the rib cage with her hard beak, shattering his ribs, sending bone splinters into his lungs and turning his internal organs into jelly. In essence, he had been hit by a five-hundred-pound battering ram, moving at almost twenty knots. He was thrown several feet into the air and, as bright red, frothing blood bubbled from his nose and mouth, he quickly died.

Oscar's partner and officer Rivera had seen enough and decided to flee the scene, only to find the *Dorado* bearing down with Joe and Rafael standing in the bow aiming shotguns at him. Two shotgun slugs ripped through the windshield of the *Santa Rosa II,* and he immediately cut his engines and surrendered.

Mortally wounded, *Lucky* was losing blood and growing weaker but still held Terry up until Joe was able to jump in and drag her back through the water to the *Dorado.* As Terry was lifted into the boat, she looked back and cried, helplessly watching as Notchka pushed the lifeless body of her son out to sea. Terry wondered, *would she ever trust humans again, after seeing her offspring brutally killed?* They fished Oscar's body out of the water and then Rafael took charge of the *Santa Rosa II* and followed Joe and Manuel in the *Dorado* back to the marina with his prisoners.

Chapter 37

Cozumel International Airport

"When will I see you again?" Terry asked Joe, as he was getting ready to board a flight to Miami.

"As soon as I can wrap up this business in New York."

Terry wasn't so sure. So much had happened in such a short period of time. Thoughts raced through her mind. *Was it real? Did it all really happen? It wasn't a dream, was it?*

"I have to make a report to the task force in Miami and then the Feds and local authorities have to figure out who gets extradited to New York, who gets tried where. A lot of suspects were taken down: drug runners between Miami and New York, employees of the cruise lines, and citizens of Mexico. It will take a while to sort it all out."

"I see," Terry said, icily. It sounded like a brush-off to her. Joe caught the tone in her voice.

"Listen, Terry. Everything that happened between us was real – our feelings, my feelings for you, are genuine. Terry, I told you that I love you and I meant it."

"So, do we have a chance, Joe? I need to know."

"Attention all passengers, final call. U.S. Airways Flight 1145 to Miami is now boarding."

"Terry, I have to run. I'll call you soon, I promise." As they embraced and kissed, Terry didn't know what to feel, what to believe. She watched Joe walk across the tarmac and, as he stepped inside the plane, Terry wondered if she would ever see him again. She thought about how he seemed to have changed during the arrest by the local strike team and immediately afterward. He had become one-hundred-percent focused on the job he had to do, the consummate professional. *Well*, she thought, *that's why he came down here, after all, not to fall in love with me.* She knew he had a job to do, a mission to accomplish.

A few minutes later, the plane accelerated down the runway and took off into the late-afternoon sun. Terry watched it until it became a mere speck in the sky, as thoughts raced through her mind. *But was I only just a means to an end? Did he just use me as an aid in his investigation?* Driving home from the airport, Terry was extremely confused and sad.

Over the next several months, Joe kept in touch with Terry by email and phone while he was in New York. She was busy with her dive operation, grateful that the hectic pace of running her business kept her from thinking too much about how much she missed Joe. In addition to his regular duties, he was busy preparing for the upcoming trials of those arrested in the drug-smuggling operation. As the trial dates grew closer and demands on his time increased, communication between them became more sporadic, although Joe tried to stay in touch as often as he could. Terry wanted to press Joe on their future, but realized this was not the time. Still, it was a conversation that she wanted to have, felt that she had earned and deserved. She couldn't help but wonder, *do we still have a future, Joe?*

One afternoon, Terry met Sergeant Rafael Gonzalez for lunch. "Have you heard the news about Joe?" he asked. She said that they had spoken a few days earlier while the trial was still underway, but not since then. Rafael showed her a copy of the *New York Times* that he had just pulled off the internet. On the front page was a story about the trial, which had concluded yesterday. The prosecutors had won convictions in the drug case and there was a picture of Joe and Bill Ryan getting medals from the Mayor of New York. Terry read about the promotion that Joe had received, and that he was now considered to be a rising star with a bright future in the NYPD. She looked closely at the picture and noticed a policewoman standing next to Joe. She also noted the admiring glance of the woman looking at Joe. Terry wondered who she was. *Does she work with Joe? Is she in love with him? Is he dating her?*

Then she glanced at a second story as a familiar name caught her eye and she found herself staring in shock at a picture showing the eyes of a shattered man in handcuffs, looking like a deer caught in the headlights. "Wow! Did you see this other story, Rafael?" Terry exclaimed.

He leaned over to read it with her. The owner of Gateway Express Trucking Company, Carl Olsen, had been indicted for his role in transporting cocaine to the Midwest for Oscar's drug ring.

Terry immediately thought of Nora, Melissa, and Tommy, and what they must be going through. She realized that her own personal problems concerning her love life paled by comparison. The story went on to say that prosecutors had set what they thought was a high enough bail to keep him in jail until the trial, but were surprised when he was able to come up with the required $1 million. "Well, Rafael, I guess they underestimated how much money he had been able to stash working with Oscar."

"I'm sure it was a substantial amount," he agreed, as their lunch was served. After coffee, Terry said, "Well, I have some diving to do this afternoon. Take care, Rafael It was good to see you. Keep in touch; don't be a stranger, stop by and see me sometime."

"I'll do that, Terry. It was good to see you, also."

Chapter 38

New York City

The head of the Federal task force to which Joe had been assigned had highly recommended Joe to his superiors for his role in breaking the drug ring and they invited him to come to Washington, D.C., for an interview with the Federal Drug Enforcement Administration. The interview had gone very well, and several days later Joe received a very attractive offer letter in the mail. In addition, the Federal Bureau of Investigation had also learned about Joe and had sent him a letter requesting an exploratory meeting to discuss possible employment as an FBI agent. Closer to home, Joe's promotion to Detective-Commander resulted in additional responsibility, along with a salary increase.

Joe realized that, as a result of everything that had happened over the past year, he now had many options. One decision that he made was not to leave the NYPD. The interest from other law enforcement agencies was enticing, but Joe realized that his heart was in law enforcement at a local level, where he felt he would have more of a direct impact on the quality of life of those around him. In addition, Joe's successful international experience had also catapulted him into the limelight among the NYPD brass. He was often consulted on police matters pertaining to international situations and was occasionally invited to be the featured speaker at functions regarding cooperation among foreign law enforcement departments.

Joe returned to his house on Long Island late one evening; it had been another long day and he was tired. He looked at the pictures of his late family on his bedroom dresser and thought about how much he missed them. Despite his professional and social success, there was a void in his life. In the solitude of his quiet and empty home, Joe reflected on the events of the past year. His prospects for a successful career had never been more promising, but he felt incomplete, unfulfilled.

Joe knew that he was at a crossroads and that he had to make some serious decisions about the direction of the rest of his life.

Chapter 39

Cozumel

Terry parked her car in front of her apartment at 4pm, after a tiring day of diving. She had given lessons to two new divers in the morning and had taken a large group of advanced divers out on a two-tank dive in the afternoon. When she entered the apartment she noticed that the message light on her answering machine indicated that she had some calls waiting.

Terry took the pad and pencil that were next to the phone and pressed the "play" button, expecting to start taking down requests from customers for future bookings. Instead, she was thrilled to hear Joe Manetta's voice. "Terry, please call me as soon as you can. It's very important!" Terry's heart skipped a beat, *Boy, he sounds excited.* "I need to talk to you, because..."

Terry never heard the rest of the message. She heard a sound behind her, but before she could turn to see what it was, the next thing Terry felt was a searing pain in the back of her head and then she collapsed into unconsciousness. A hand reached down and tore the phone line from the wall.

Terry came to after a few minutes and, through a haze, noticed the phone wire dangling from the wall and remembered that she had been listening to a message, *From... Joe? Was he here? Where am I? What happ...* She tried to sit up, but the pain in her head returned and she rolled over. She groaned, holding the back of her head and tried again. When the fog cleared Terry managed to sit up and she found herself staring into the face of... Carl Olsen! She blinked, shook her head and the shock of recognition helped her to regain full consciousness.

His eyes bore no resemblance to the scared, deer-in-the-headlights look that she remembered seeing in the newspaper picture some months back. Instead, he had the crazed look of someone who had gone over the edge of sanity, into madness. For a moment she thought that the spirit of Oscar had taken possession of Carl Olsen's body. "What the... what are *you* doing here?" was all she could say, weakly.

"I escaped, jumped bail, just before my trial started, and now I'm heading to South America. No way I'm going to rot in some prison cell for the rest of my life. But I came here to take care of you first!" Terry just stared at him blankly; partly in shock that this was happening to her and partly trying to assess her situation and her options. "You and your fucking cop-boyfriend ruined my life, but you're going to pay," he yelled at her, voice rising. She tried to talk to him to buy time, to figure out a plan.

"Carl, I never knew that you were involved. I'm really sorry for the trouble that you and your family are in, if I can help you in any..."

"Shut up!" he screamed, so loudly that Terry flinched. "I'm outta here, but first I'm putting a bullet in your head," he said as he raised his hand and Terry stared into the barrel of a .45 automatic, paralyzed with fear, realizing finally that she was going to die. "I could have shot you when you walked in, but I wanted to see the terror and pain in your face when I kill you."

Terry realized that deep inside, Carl Olsen was a lot more like Oscar than she or anyone else would have ever thought possible.

Carl continued to rale, "I lost everything because of you – my business, my money, my future, all the millions that I was going to make, everything!" He started to squeeze the trigger and Terry turned away, squeezing her eyes shut, waiting to feel the bullet tear through her flesh. *Your life really does flash before your eyes,* was her last thought before she heard the deafening roar of the gun. Her body shuddered, she felt herself covered in warm blood, and then felt pain as a crushing weight fell on top of her, but then rolled off.

Terry opened her eyes. *Wait, how can I do that if I'm dead?* and was startled to see a body lying next to her and the bloody pulp of what had been Carl Olsen's face inches from her own face.

She turned and looked where Carl had been standing and saw, in the open doorway, Sergeant Rafael Gonzalez, still in a two-handed shooter's stance, his own police-issue automatic weapon still smoking from the single shot that he had expertly placed into the back of Carl Olsen's head, and which had exited, blowing his face away.

Terry sat on the floor, soaked in Carl's blood, in a daze, her mind trying to assimilate what had just happened. Rafael walked over, helped her to her feet and then quickly into a chair as her legs buckled. She looked at him, questioning him with her eyes, but not yet able to formulate words. "Joe couldn't reach you, so after he left you a message on your machine he called me this morning. He told me that Carl Olsen was reported missing yesterday, had probably fled the county, and that there was a chance he could be coming to Mexico. I emailed a photo to the immigration people at the airport and someone recognized his picture as someone who had entered Cozumel earlier today but under a different name. I rushed over as soon as I could."

Rafael could see that Terry was still in shock, not really comprehending what he was saying. He smiled and said, "Besides, several months ago, when we had lunch, did you not invite me to stop by and visit you sometime?"

The sudden humor broke through Terry's shock and she embraced him tightly, half sobbing, half laughing as her tension was released in a flood of conflicting emotions.

"It's over, Rafael. It's finally over."

Epilogue

Cozumel,

One Year Later

The *Dorado* cut through the water, throwing up a large wake as it veered toward the pier next to the Palancar Princess hotel. As it slowed and Pepe prepared to tie the boat up to the pier, Terry waved to the family waiting for her. "Hi, Terry," shouted Nora Olsen. "It's wonderful to see you again!"

"I'm so glad that you decided to come back," Terry said, hugging Nora as she boarded the boat. "I've been worried about you and the children; how are you all coping?" she asked with genuine concern.

Nora embraced her back, "Oh, Terry. I'm so sorry about what Carl... are you OK?"

"Yes, it was a close call, and I guess I was just very lucky, but I'm fine now, Nora. Besides, it wasn't your fault."

"Well, it's been a difficult year for us, but my folks have been a big help. We'll make it. Carl was a basically good man, but he just got into a situation that was over his head."

"I know," said Terry, supportively, but privately thinking, *how well did you really know your husband, Nora?* "Oscar ruined a lot of lives, but at least he won't be doing that to anyone else, ever again."

"Thank God! I tried to warn Carl to stay away from him, but..." Nora's voice trailed off.

As Manuel and Pepe secured the lines, Melissa jumped aboard. Now sixteen, she had an even larger group of admirers than last year. "Hi, Miss Hunter," she said.

"Well, Melissa, my name is Terry *Manetta* now. I'd like you to meet my husband and dive partner, Joe."

"Oh how wonderful," said Nora, hugging Terry and then Joe. "Now you take good care of her, Joe."

"Thanks, Nora. You bet I will, but she already informed me that, underwater, she's the boss."

"And don't you forget it, mister," said Terry, playfully giving Joe a sharp jab in the ribs.

Nora, caught in the spirit of the exchange, rolled her eyes as Joe winced in pain. "Oh, I can see this will be a long and very interesting relationship!"

"Congratulations to both of you," said Melissa, very properly.

As they prepared to leave for the reef, they looked for Tommy, who was standing at the other end of the pier, intently watching the scuba tanks being filled, mesmerized, as always, listening to the hissing of compressed air and the banging and clanking of the tanks as they were rolled out to the waiting dive boats. Nora yelled to him, "Hey, Tommy, come on. We're leaving now!" Tommy ran the length of the pier and jumped onto the boat as Manuel was revving up the motors. He caught his breath and then he noticed Joe standing next to Terry and looked at him with a quizzical expression.

"Tommy, I'd like you to meet my husband, Joe. We were married only a few months ago."

"Well, dear, what do you say?" prompted Tommy's mother. Tommy extended his hand to Joe, and then looked at Terry with the broadest grin she had ever seen on a little boy.

"Awesome!"

"Why, thank you, Thomas," Terry said, as she laughed and playfully mussed Tommy's hair with her hand.

She casually glanced over his shoulder as the *Dorado* moved out into the channel, when a sudden movement in the water caught her eye. She looked out about fifty yards from the boat and saw the dorsal fins of two dolphins slicing through the water, toward a group of snorkelers swimming next to a catamaran. Melissa called out, "Look, it's Notchka!" Terry looked more carefully; she hadn't seen Notchka in over a year and wondered what had happened to her. Sure enough, Terry recognized the telltale notch in the fluke. She also noticed that the second dorsal fin was much smaller and a lump rose in her throat as she realized that the other dolphin was a very young calf.

It *was* Notchka and she was escorting her new calf to play with the snorkelers. Terry watched the scene unfold through tears in her eyes, but, for a change, they were tears of joy as she marveled at the trust of the mother dolphin. Notchka was giving humans a second chance.

As the young dolphin, only several months old, swam around and through the group of snorkelers, mostly children, Notchka swam close by, looking on, protectively but approvingly. Joe stepped over next to Terry and they put their arms around each other as they watched the two dolphins interact with the snorkelers. "Well, that is really something!" was all he could say.

Terry smiled and, as she squeezed him affectionately, said, "No, Joe, *that's* truly awesome!

* * *

Note: The photographs in this book are also available as beautiful 8 x 10 color glossy prints, suitable for framing. For details, contact the author directly at: pjmila@hotmail.com

Coming Next Year: *WHALES' ANGELS*

Terry and Joe Manetta are building a life together, running their dive operation in Cozumel, Mexico, while trying to start a family. Over dinner one evening with one of their dive customers, Femke Van der Zee, from the Netherlands, they learn where it is possible to free-dive with humpback whales.

Terry and Joe are off on another undersea adventure, traveling to the waters of the Silver Bank in the Dominican Republic to swim with humpback whales. Their emotionally moving encounters with humpback mother whales and their newborn calves sensitize Joe and Terry to the plight of all the great whales, especially when they learn that Japan, Finland, Norway and Iceland are conspiring to overturn the International Whaling Commission's ban on commercial whaling.

When they learn that pirate whalers are killing not only whales, but also members of an anti-whaling conservation organization, they contact the group to find out how they can help. But their involvement enmeshes them in a dark world of international politics, intrigue, and murder.

Look for *Whales' Angels,* in early 2005.

About the Author

Paul J. Mila retired after a successful career in corporate life, and now devotes his time to writing, scuba diving and underwater photography. He has enjoyed the opportunity to photograph and dive with Caribbean reef sharks in the Bahamas, humpback whales in the Dominican Republic, and an amazing variety of sea life in Cozumel and Bonaire.

His underwater pictures have been featured on web sites related to scuba diving and have been shown at the recent, *Mind Body Spirit Festival* in Australia. He is a N.A.U.I. certified advanced diver and has a P.A.D.I. certification as an Underwater Naturalist.

In pursuing a writing career, he has followed the advice of writers who said to write about what you know and like. Consequently, he has incorporated the ocean and diving as the core of his writing. Diving in the same waters as the characters in his book has enabled him to write with realism, and to describe in an interesting fashion for the non-diving reader what it feels like to explore our undersea world.

He and his family reside in Carle Place, New York, a small town on Long Island.

Printed in the United States
17532LVS00002B/154-162